OUT OF THE BLUE

THE WEIGHT OF THE BADGE – BOOK THREE

KAYLEE ROSE

D1507130

RED'S BOOKSHELF PUBLISHING

Red's Bookshelf Publishing

Out of the Blue: The Weight of the Badge – Book Three

www.authorkayleerose.com

Ordering Information:

Quantity sales. Special discounts are available on quantity purchases by corporations, associations, and others. For details, contact the "Special Sales Department" at the address above.

OOTBTWOTBBT / Kaylee Rose – 1st Ed.

❀ Created with Vellum

He's not just a man in uniform.

He's my hero, my best friend, and the love of my life.

He's my husband.

~

The Weight of the Badge series is dedicated to the men and women in the first responder family.

Thank you for protecting and caring for our communities.

Please don't forget to take care of yourselves, too.

Come home safe.

TRISH

Walking away from the playground with Rory's hand in mine, I grin at how easy it was to pull off my plan.

Lance and Kellie were too preoccupied with their little lovefest to notice me, oblivious to the danger I pose. Coaxing Rory away from the other children was hands down the most devious idea I've ever had. Who knew the stuffed bunny I gave her while shopping with her grandmother all those weeks ago would be the perfect catalyst for my scheme?

Kellie underestimated me, but that won't be the case after today. She will always wonder how this would have turned out if only she was paying attention.

The same goes for Lance. He should have learned his lesson after Paul. We are soulmates, destined to be, and no matter who stands in the way, I'm his, and he's mine. Of course, he's still not aware of my part in Paul's suicide. It was simple, really. A few harsh words about his dead wife as he was leaving Heath's did the trick. I may as well have been there when he pulled the trigger.

After his death, the path back into Lance's arms should

have been straightforward. Lance was mine for the taking, but then Kellie wormed her way into his life.

But that was then, and this is now.

I can't help thinking Kellie stole what should have been mine. Lance and I could be so happy if only he'd let me back in.

There's no doubt that after today, he'll fully understand that Kellie can never be the woman to make him happy. She's too wrapped up in herself and Rory to see what I finally see—the man behind the badge.

Unfortunately, my plan has taken longer than I intended it to, but everything is coming together perfectly. If destroying Kellie's world is what it takes to get Lance back, then that's exactly what I'll do. She has the most important person in my life, and now, I have hers.

"Trish, where are the bunnies?" Rory's question interrupts my plan to reunite with Lance.

"Hmm, they were right over there earlier." I adopt a cutesy voice and point to a fallen log a few steps away.

"I can't see any." The little brat is too clever for her own good.

"Then I guess we need to keep looking." I tug on her hand harder than necessary, causing her to stumble.

"Addy K's gonna be mad." Rory pulls away. She looks over her shoulder, but we are too deep into the woods for her to see anything through the trees. For a preschooler, she seems more aware of her surroundings than I expected.

"Why would you think that, sweetie?" I almost choke on the syrupy sweet voice oozing from my lips in an attempt to keep her calm.

"She said to stay where she could see me." Rory bites her lip and shakes her head. She's an innocent pawn but a necessary casualty for me to carry out my mission.

"But that was before she told me to take you to see the

bunnies. Remember, Addy K and Lance are my friends." I keep walking, hoping to get farther into hiding before Kellie and Lance notice Rory is no longer playing with her friends.

Flashes of Lance snuggled up with Kellie under the tree has my stomach in knots. No woman wants to see the man she loves in the arms of another. If I didn't know any better, I'd swear Kellie was flaunting her hold on Lance in my face. Mocking me as if she'd won. It makes me realize one thing; I need to get Kellie out of the picture now and before Lance falls deeper into her tangled web. He loves me, not her.

"Let's go. We're almost there, but we need to go faster, or we won't get to see the mamma and her babies." I growl through clenched teeth, sounding less like Mary Poppins and more like Cruella De Vil. She isn't making this easy, and my patience is fading fast.

"I'm trying, but you're too fast," Rory whines like a spoiled brat.

"Just a little farther." I flash her my warmest smile. "I think I hear them." Holding out my hand to her, she takes it, and we walk deeper into the grove of redwood trees. "Don't forget, we have to stay super quiet, or we'll scare them away."

Rory's lip quivers and unshed tears fill her eyes. She pulls her hand out of mine. Shivering, she wraps her arms around her little body.

"I'm cold. I want Addy K?" We are deep in the forest now and the giant trees block out the sun's rays.

Faintly, I can hear people calling Rory's name. *Fuck! They've figured out she's missing sooner than I planned.*

My mind races as I think of a new way to get Rory away from here. I could pick her up and run, but we are still too close to the park, and someone may hear her if she screams.

We stop by a tree stump, and I kneel, now eye to eye with Rory. "I know, I have an idea. Maybe Aunt Kellie will let you keep one of the bunnies. Wouldn't that be great?" She doesn't answer. "I bet your new kitty, Tigress, will love having a playmate."

Rory places her thumb into her mouth and blinks back her tears.

"Rory! Where are you?" A booming male voice shouts and she turns her head.

"Hurry up. We need to go now!"

"Addy K!" Rory shouts and runs away from me.

"Get back here," I snarl. "You little bitch!"

She's scared of me. I see it in her eyes. "Go away." Rory screams. "Addy K! Lance!"

As she runs, I jump to my feet, ready to give chase, only to trip on a tree root. "Son of a bitch." I hit the ground with a thud as pain shoots up from my ankle to the top of my leg. Breathless, I roll onto my back.

"Rory! Can you hear me?" It's Lance's voice. I'd know it anywhere.

Gingerly, I force myself to my feet and hobble as fast as possible to the dirt path that leads up to the back road where I parked the car. I was so close and now all I can do is try to get away without being seen.

2

LANCE

Standing at the edge of the playground, where I last saw Rory, I scan the area carefully, mentally categorizing faces in the crowd and the places she could be hiding.

My lungs burn from screaming her name repeatedly while running through the park. "Rory! Can you hear me?" I shout as my eyes dart around the open space, hoping to catch a glimpse of her. *Where the hell is she?* "Rory!"

My phone buzzes in my hand. It's the call I've been waiting for.

"Jackson…"

"Any sign of her, Lance?"

"No! Have they found anything on the park security cameras?"

"Not yet, but they're still trying to get access to the rec building." I hear the rev of his engine and siren in the background.

"Fuck, we don't have time for this. Tell them to break the God damn door down if they have to."

"You need to step out of your head for a minute and think

like a cop and not the victim." Jackson's stern tone puts me in check.

"I know. I know, fuck." My fingers hurt from squeezing my phone and pressing it against my ear. "Tell me what to do. Our little girl is missing, and my girlfriend is a complete mess." I pace the length of the narrow path beside the play structure. "I'm losing my mind."

Jackson tries to calm me down. "Dispatch has every available officer on alert. You know how this works. It's never as fast as we want it to be. And right now…" he pauses, "you have to pull yourself together for Kellie's sake. She needs you to be her strength now more than ever."

Rubbing my hand roughly over the back of my neck, I feel sweat coat my palm and silently berate myself. *How could I be so stupid?* I've heard hundreds of horror stories about a child being there one minute and gone the next but never imagined it would happen to somebody I love.

"It's my fault…"

"Stop. This isn't the time for you to give up and feel sorry for yourself. Pull your head out of your ass right now and man the fuck up."

I allow his words to sink in, letting them light a fire inside me. He's right. I'm angry at myself for allowing someone to take Rory right under my nose, and I hate that I can't do a fucking thing about it, but the irrational way I'm acting isn't productive.

I try to push away my doubts and move on to what needs to be done. First, we get Rory back, then I find the person who did this and make them pay.

"Alright. I got it. When are we looking at getting more officers out here?"

"Sarge has called for mutual aid from surrounding cities. ETA is less than five minutes."

"Just get them here, Jackson. I can't lose another person I love."

"You know I won't let that happen." His confidence is reassuring.

"Just hurry. I'm waiting near the playground." I disconnect the call and shove it into my back pocket.

Kellie is just steps away from me, pleading with another group of adults, trying to find any sign of where Rory might be or who took her.

"Have you seen my little girl? Her name is Rory." Kellie turns her cell phone for the group to see, I assume showing them one of Rory's pictures.

One of the women shakes her head slowly and continues walking down the path. Kellie turns to me before looking up to the sky and crying out once more, "Rory!" Her painful wail pierces my heart.

Heaving sobs render her useless, so I go to her, and she steps into my open arms. I pull her tightly against my chest, hoping to give her an ounce of comfort and, if I'm being honest, take some from her as well.

Our emotions are all over the place, but I'm concerned she's on the edge of breaking down, physically and mentally. Her cheeks are red and tearstained. With her warm body still snug against my chest, I ask, "Did you call your mom and dad?"

"Yes, and they said they would call your parents and get here as soon as possible." She leans away slightly, but I keep my arms wrapped protectively around her as she wipes away the tears cascading down her cheeks. Kellie's eyes remain downcast and her shoulders slump forward. "I promised my family I would take care of Rory. I've failed and now I don't know what to do? Help me." Her body feels heavy in my arms as if she's finally given into the severity of the situation.

Kellie's agonizing cry for help cuts deep. I give myself this brief moment to release my own fears and allow the pain to escape my body with each tear I shed.

Placing my lips close to her ear, I whisper, "I'll find her, I promise."

I'm not religious, but today I pray hard, willing to make a deal with the devil if necessary, hoping this will all be over soon.

God, please let me find Rory safe. I'll trade my life for hers if I have to. Just bring her home safe and sound.

With every ounce of strength I can muster, I raise my chin and choke down my emotions. Standing here crying won't bring Rory home. I blow out a breath to prepare for my next move. It's time for me to flip the switch from the man whose child is missing and take control of my actions from the outside as I would while on duty.

Knowing Kellie isn't going to like what I have to say, I tighten my hold on her. "Kel, we need to make a plan. The deputies will be here in a few minutes. Until then, we need to stay right here and remain as calm as possible."

She fights against my hold, trying to push away. "Let go!" she hisses her words and shoves against my chest harder. When I open my arms, she stumbles back a step and glares at me. "You expect me to just stand here and wait for them? Are you fucking kidding me?"

"You need to listen to me. I want to speed up the process as much as you do, but it's not how this works."

Kellie's eyes narrow and she speaks through clenched teeth. "You told me she'd be okay by herself. I trusted you."

"I know. I fucked up, but this isn't the time. Jackson will be here any minute and..."

"Rory could be anywhere by now. We can't wait for Jackson. We have to keep searching."

I'm not going to argue with her. I lower my voice, instinctively trying to deescalate the situation. "Listen to me. I've already called dispatch and set the wheels in motion for an AMBER Alert. This will send out the alarm of a missing child considered to be in immediate danger. Until the deputies get here, there isn't much else we can do."

Kellie scowls at me. "You're wrong. There's plenty we can do. Every corner of this park, every house surrounding it, and every single fucking car needs to be searched, but no, you want to stand here like Rory isn't in any danger?"

"But we can't do any of that if all we do is run around in circles." I'm careful to keep my voice low but assertive while I try to hide my own frustration and fears.

"Why are you so calm? Do you even care that Rory is missing?" She shoots daggers at me as if I'm the villain.

Her words are wounding, causing me to take two steps back. I know she's taking her anger out on me and deserve it for not exercising better judgment, but I'm still stunned.

"Do you really think I don't care?" I lash out without thinking. "I'm holding my shit together on a razor-thin line, trying to stay in control long enough to do my job and get Rory back."

"Fine then." She puts her hands on my chest and shoves hard. "Do your fucking job and find Rory!" Her voice is hoarse now, barely audible from yelling so much. She turns and runs toward another family nearby, frantically asking if they saw anything. I keep a close eye on her, knowing how fragile she is, but keep my distance as to not upset her more.

Kellie continues her frantic search and stumbles when stepping around one of the horseshoe pits. Her pace is slowing down, exhaustion catching up to her. She pauses, hands on her knees, breathing heavily. An elderly man guides her to sit on a nearby bench and gives her a bottle of water. Knowing she is being cared for affords me a chance to switch my focus back to what I need to do for Rory.

Deep down, I know she wouldn't have wandered off on

her own. My gut says this isn't a stranger abduction with so many people around. There's only one person I can think of that would have the nerve to cause this much panic, but she's not supposed to be anywhere near here or us.

The sound of police sirens fills the air.

Jackson is the first to arrive. He parks at an angle that blocks the parking lot exit, keeping cars from leaving without being searched. Jackson slams the car door and runs in my direction.

Kellie rushes to Jackson, clutching at his uniform. "Jackson! She was right here. Someone had to have seen something."

Jackson pulls Kellie into a hug. This isn't just another call for him either; it's his family too. When he releases her, I see his professional expression return: the one we use to keep the emotional distance when necessary, but his voice cracks, betraying him while speaking. "Kellie, please, you need to calm down." He swallows hard and removes a pen and notebook from his breast pocket. "I need to get some information from you. Let's start at the beginning. What was she wearing?"

"A pink shirt and shorts, sandals, and her hair is in ponytails." Although I've shown Jackson a few pictures of Rory, he's never met her, so Kellie rattles off her basic description. Age, height, weight, and complexion.

"Hang on, I'll send you the picture I took today while she was playing." I pause for just a second when I see Rory's smiling face on my screen, then snap back into action, forwarding the picture to Jackson's phone.

He turns his head and speaks into the mic on his shoulder, relaying Rory's information for dispatch to send out.

Kellie turns in a circle, anxiously searching the park for the millionth time. "How long is this going to take?" She throws up her arms and huffs out an exasperated breath.

"Now we have to wait for dispatch to give us more information." Kellie glares at me again.

Jackson takes control and continues with his questions, addressing me now. "Alright, the others should be here any minute. Where have you searched?" He and I discuss the places we've looked.

"Hurry up! By the time you two finish talking, Rory could be anywhere." Kellie fumes while her eyes continue to scan the park and its surroundings.

"Okay, once everyone arrives, we can set up teams and widen the search." Jackson puts the small notebook back into his breast pocket.

Kellie suddenly explodes with rage. "I'm not waiting any longer. You can stand here and talk about it, but I need to keep searching for my baby." She sprints away from us towards the basketball hoops and brick recreation building.

When Jackson turns to follow her, I put my hand on his arm to stop him. "You have to find Rory. I can't lose them."

"We'll find her. I promise." This time I do believe him, refusing to have negative thoughts.

Before we can follow Kellie, three more deputies arrive. Jackson briefs them on the situation and sends a group text with Rory's picture. I listen to them strategize but try to keep my eyes on Kellie too. With a plan to cover the area, the deputies disperse to their assigned section of the park.

3

KELLIE

"Rory! Where are you? Addy K can't see you!" I scream, ignoring the painful burning in my throat. Running aimlessly, hoping I'll find someone who saw Rory leave the playground, has me out of breath, but I refuse to slow down.

How could I take my eyes off the one person that relies on me to keep her safe?

The acid in my stomach churns as I think of who might have taken her and why?

Oh, God, please no!

I bend over and gag just thinking about what she might be going through. Was she snatched by some opportunistic pervert–someone that saw her unaccompanied by an adult and took their chance maybe? Terror courses through me because I know Rory will be confused and scared. Is she calling out to me to save her? Is she lying hurt somewhere and unable to get back to me?

My fists ball up so tight that my nails cut into my palms. If whoever has taken her hurts her, I'll make them pay with their lives. The more my mind wanders to the unthinkable, the faster I breathe. A panic attack threatens to disable me, but I fight to slow my breathing before I pass out.

Not now, Kellie. You need to stay in control and find Rory.

This park is huge but not so big a child can disappear into thin air. In my heart, I feel Rory is still close by. Though I didn't give birth to her, the bond I have with her is strong, like any mother and daughter.

I tell myself she's not far away, but what if I'm wrong and it's my mind trying to prepare me for the worst?

What will I do if she never comes home again?

Knock it off! I tell myself. *They'll find her!*

I battle internally to push away the negative thoughts and remain positive. "Rory, can you hear me?" I yell, my throat hoarse from screaming.

Running my fingers through my hair, I pull on it in frustration. I'm in a crowded park, surrounded by people but so far, nobody saw Rory leave the playground. The playground is empty now and parents have their children huddled protectively near them.

Turning slowly, I cup my hands around my mouth and shout as loud as possible, "Has anyone seen my little girl? She's wearing a pink shirt, sandals and has ponytails in her hair."

"I'm so sorry, I haven't seen her," answers a woman close to me. "How can we help?"

"Honestly, I'm not sure." Looking around, I feel overwhelmed and utterly useless. The park and the surrounding hiking trails cover several acres. There are so many places she could be. As curious as Rory is, it's possible that she wandered off and just got lost. *Don't give up, Kellie. Rory is counting on you.* "There is still a lot of places that haven't been searched yet. Maybe we can spread out."

"I'll look behind the tennis courts," a woman says and dashes off.

"What about the grove of redwood trees? Has anyone gone there?" Another person asks.

"That's where I'm going next." Even though I've told Rory to stay away from the trees, doing the opposite would be completely normal.

"We'll take the trails by the old church while you check the grove." A young couple run away to start their search.

"Please keep looking until Rory is found and if you see anything unusual, call 911."

The small group of adults leave to scour the park. With so many people searching, I have to believe she will be found soon. Taking two steps in the direction of the trees, my calf muscles cramp, causing me to fall to the ground in agony. "Ow. Fuck."

I try stretching and pointing my toes, but it only hurts more. Sitting up, I use my thumbs to massage the painful knot that has formed in my leg. Tipping my head back, I look to the heavens, and beg for divine intervention. "Leslie, if you're listening, I need you now, more than ever." If there is a Heaven, please help me. "Rory needs you to keep her safe." Tears fall down my cheeks. "Bring our baby home."

Wiping away the tears, I force myself to stand and hobble over to the nearby bench for support. The ache in my leg is nothing compared to the one in my chest. A quick glance over my shoulder to where Lance and Jackson were standing earlier gives me a sliver of hope. Several men and women in uniform surround them as they appear to be going over the plan I was too impatient to wait for.

When the group breaks apart and begins their search, Lance looks over to me, holding my gaze for just a moment before turning his back. I have no doubt he's disgusted with the way I treated him. The instant my ruthless words were said, I regretted them. Questioning his love for Rory was beyond cruel and nothing I can say will ever take it back.

The blame lies firmly at my feet, yet I took out my anger on him.

Lance is the one person I should be leaning on for support and I stupidly pushed him away. He may be angry at me, but I know that won't stop him from finding Rory. Regardless of what I said, Lance is a great officer. If anyone is going to find her, it will be him.

I need to gather my strength if I want to continue searching. After a few steps, my head starts to throb, and a wave of nausea has me doubled over. Grasping the sides of my head, I squeeze hard, hoping the counter pressure will relieve the pounding in my temples.

"Honey? Maybe you should sit back down." Too light-headed to stand to my full height, I turn my head in the direction of the woman's voice. Her long silver hair is twisted into a braid and draped over her shoulder. She wears a loose-fitting purple dress, along with several layers of eclectic beads, reminding me of a traveler I once saw on a crazy reality show.

"You don't understand. I can't rest. My little girl is missing."

"But dear, if you pass out, how will you be of any help to her?"

Blowing out a steadying breath, I slowly force myself to stand upright, hoping I don't topple over. Using my hand to shield the sun helps block some of the bright light, but it doesn't stop the tiny black spots I see dancing before my eyes. The swirling movement is making me even woozier.

"At least drink some water." She removes a bottle from her hobo-style purse and holds it out to me, silently insisting I take it.

I give in and accept her kind offer. My body is zapped of all energy, and I struggle to twist the top off. She takes it from me, opening it with ease. "Thank you."

"My pleasure, dear."

I'm thirstier than I realize and gulp down about half the bottle, then pour some into my hand to splash on my face. "Thank you again. I really needed that."

"No need to thank me. I can't imagine what you're going through. Has there been any sign of your daughter?"

"Nothing yet, so I'm sure you understand I need to keep looking. Thanks for the water." Before I can rush away, she reaches for my hand and envelopes it between both of hers.

"Your daughter's name is Rory, correct?"

"Yes."

"Rory is a beautiful name. Do you mind if I say a quick prayer for her return?"

I'm still not sure this woman isn't a crackpot, but I'm willing to try just about anything if it means finding Rory. "Please, continue."

"Please, God, send your angels down to watch over little Rory. Wrap her up in your love and keep her safe from those who wish to do her harm."

Stunned by her prayer, I simply nod.

"Continue to have faith and I'm certain she will be returned to you unharmed."

Overcome with emotions, I'm only able to whisper. "I hope so."

I watch as she turns away to continue down the path and realize what she just did for me. Our brief encounter has allowed me to slow down and collect myself. I feel less out of control and need to find Lance so I can be part of the search party instead of trying to do this alone.

A vendor with a pushcart rings his bell. Children from all angles stop what they are doing and rush over to see what is being sold. It looks like cotton candy and other sweets. Anxiously, I push my way through to the front, closely examining the faces of each child, hoping Rory is one of them. But unfortunately, she isn't there.

An idea springs to mind. Perhaps she is just playing hide and seek, and the temptation of candy will draw her out from her hiding spot. "Rory, hurry! Come look! Addy K has your favorite blue cotton candy." I wait and hope for an answer. "I'll buy you as many as you want if you just come here." I'm grasping at straws for any sign that she is okay. "You better hurry up before all the candy is gone." Turning in circles, there's still no sign of her.

"Where the fuck is she." The children gasp and a few shocked parents turn to glare at me. "I'm sorry, it's just…"

Before I can apologize for my foul language, a splash of pink catches my attention—a little girl with ponytails holding hands with a woman walking away from the playground.

With every ounce of energy I can pull from my fatigued body, I sprint to her and cry out, "Stop! Rory!" Reaching out, I grab the woman's shoulder and spin her around.

"Excuse me?" The woman sneers.

I stare open-mouthed and ready to verbally attack this woman for taking my child, but then the bottom drops out from my stomach when I recognize it is not my niece. "Oh, my God. I'm so sorry. I thought she was my little girl. She's missing."

Her expression softens and she lifts the child into her arms. "Oh, no! When did you last see her?"

"I don't know how long it's been… It feels like hours, but I know it hasn't been that long." Reaching into my pocket to show her a picture of Rory on my phone, my hands shake, and I struggle to enter my password. "This is her. Have you seen her?"

"No, I'm sorry, I haven't."

"If you see anything unusual, please call 911."

"I will, I promise." A tear slides down her cheek. "I hope you find her soon."

"Me too." Watching the little girl with her mom as they walk away from me cuts through my heart. She's safe in her mom's arms, just as Rory should be in mine.

I race towards another section of the park I don't remember searching earlier. Sprinting over to the edge of the basketball courts, my eyes sweep over the area. A small group of young children are drawing pictures with chalk, and a group of high school boys are playing basketball. Still, there is no sign of Rory.

A short time ago, everything was normal. It was just another beautiful day at the park with families enjoying the warm fresh air. Now it's turned to chaos as several people have begun helping with the search.

Standing still, allowing my gaze to travel over the open space, I feel my body sway. Sweat coats my skin as the sun's heat reflects the rays off the asphalt, upping the temperature, but for some reason, I feel goosebumps cover my arms, making me shiver.

"I won't stop searching… Rory." My words sound jumbled in my head. Another step and my legs buckle, causing me to stumble over my feet. Before crashing to the ground, I reach out and grasp the metal pole used for the basketball hoop. My vision is clouded, and I hear a ringing in my ears.

"Ma'am, are you okay?" A deep voice asks.

"I don't… " I try to talk between gasps. "I think I'm going to …" I choke down the bile threatening to climb up my throat. "It hurts to breathe." My head tilts back as my vision fades away.

Voices penetrate the darkness as I feel someone gently shake my shoulder.

"Ma'am. Can you hear me?" I open my mouth to reply,

but nothing comes out. My vision is fuzzy, and I can't focus on the person talking to me.

"Jimmy, go get those cops over there."

Groggy and confused, I ask, "What happened?"

"I think you fainted." A cold cloth is swiped over my cheeks before being placed on my forehead.

"How long was I out?" Pain like I've never felt before radiates throughout my entire body, and the pounding in my head suggests I may have hit the ground.

"Less than a minute." Another cool compress replaces the now warm one on my forehead, but I pull it off.

"I need to go–can't stop looking." My feeble attempt to sit up is halted by a set of strong hands holding me still.

"Ma'am, you really need to stay here until the ambulance arrives. You don't look very good."

"You don't understand…" I desperately claw at the guy's T-shirt, pleading with him to let me keep searching for Rory. "I need to keep looking."

"Please, Ma'am…" Too tired to fight, I finally give in and stare up at the sky. My eyes follow the path of the clouds circling overhead, making me dizzier than I already feel. "Leslie… help me."

I hear heavy footsteps approaching and more voices, but nothing they say is making sense.

With one last cry for help, I plead with anyone who might be listening. "You have to find Rory." It's the only thing I can manage to say before everything fades to black.

4

LANCE

"Hey! Are you the guy looking for the missing kid?" An out of breath young man rushes toward us, interrupting Jackson and me.

"Yeah, why?" I ask.

"You need to get over there quick." He points to the basketball courts, where a small group has gathered. A wave of fear zips through me when hearing the urgency in his voice.

"What is it?" Jackson asks while peering over his shoulder.

"She's lying on the ground and needs an ambulance," he says, trying to catch his breath.

"Fuck! Rory!" *Please, God, let her be okay.*

"Let's go!" Jackson's words snap me back to the present.

Reaching the basketball courts, I see the circle of onlookers blocking our path. Impatiently, I push past them, not knowing what I will find. "Get out of my way!" My body stiffens when I see Kellie lying in a crumpled heap on the ground. She has no color in her cheeks, nor is she moving. "Jackson! Call for an ambulance now," I shout. Her eyes are closed, but I see the rise and fall of her chest, so I know she's breathing.

"On it." I hear him talking into his radio and wait for his response. "ETA is five minutes."

"Let them know she's breathing but unconscious."

Jackson relays the information to dispatch then turns to the bystanders. "Did anyone see anything?"

"I did." A young man holding a basketball approaches cautiously. "She was asking if anybody had seen her daughter and then just sort of passed out. Her head hit the ground pretty hard."

"This can't be happening right now," I grumble under my breath but don't take my eyes off Kellie. Sliding my fingers along her neck, I check her pulse. Her heart rate is slow but steady.

"Is she dead?" I look up and shoot daggers at the woman craning her neck to secure a better view.

"Ma'am, you need to step back." Jackson handles her before I say or do something I might regret.

I check my watch. "Damn it! Jackson, what's taking the ambulance so long?"

"They're coming, Lance. Just focus on Kellie right now." Jackson kneels on the opposite side of Kellie, facing me. I note the furrow in his. "How's she doing?"

I lift her limp hand, placing it against my cheek, and notice how clammy her palm feels. "I just want her to open her eyes."

"Okay, I'll let dispatch know there is no change and get an up-to-date ETA." Jackson pushes himself to his feet then walks a few steps away while speaking into his mic.

"Kellie, please wake up." I shake her shoulder gently. "Come on, baby, open your eyes for me."

She whispers something, but I can't understand what she's trying to say. "What is it, Sweetheart? I can't hear you." I lean in, and she mumbles again, but I can't catch her words. The noise from the multitude of bystanders surrounding us makes it even more difficult to understand what she is trying to say.

"Lance, the ambulance is pulling up now."

A sense of relief sweeps through me but looking up at Jackson, I notice a woman with her phone pointed directly at Kellie and me.

"Get them out of here now," I growl from between gritted teeth while trying my best to control my rage. I move my body and use it as a shield to protect Kellie from their prying eyes. This isn't a show for them to gawk at and stream live on Facebook.

"Alright. I need everyone to back up and get out of here. We have this under control." Gradually, people move away to a more respectable distance. A few more deputies have arrived on the scene and help disperse the crowd.

I return my attention back to Kellie. "Come on, babe. Open your eyes?" Running my hands up and down her arms, I realize I've forgotten my basic first responder training. It's only when I see the goosebumps covering the skin on her arms that I realize she's cold. Pulling off my hoodie, I cover her, then sweep the wisps of hair from her forehead. I angle my body to block out the sun, casting a shadow over her face.

"Lance…" Kellie blinks a few times, then slowly opens her eyes. She tries to push up on her elbows but collapses under her own weight.

"Try not to move." I place my hand on her shoulder.

"What happened?" She touches a spot on her head and grimaces.

"You passed out and hit your head. You need to stay where you are." Brushing her hair to the side, I see a lump above her temple, but thankfully, there's no blood.

"Where's Rory?" Kellie asks in a raspy voice. She tosses the jacket covering her aside and looks around.

"We haven't found her yet, but we will."

"Help me up. We need to keep looking." She struggles against my hold, but I keep my hand firmly on her shoulders, refusing to let her up.

"Stop. You hit your head and need to get checked out first."

"There's nothing wrong with me." She shakes her head, then squeezes her eyes tight shut, wincing in pain from even the slightest of movement. I know she's hurting emotionally and physically, but just as any mother would do, she's putting Rory first.

"You're not alright. Just tell me what hurts."

"Fine." She snaps at me. "There's some pain behind my eyes, but I'll be okay. Rory is all that matters."

"That's not true. You both matter to me." Cupping her cheek, I use my thumb to brush away a stray tear. "You and Rory are my world and I'd be lost without both of you in it."

"But I can't just lay here when Rory is out there. She could be hurt, or worse."

Indecision grabs hold, ripping me in two. My need to find Rory is just as strong as remaining here to care for Kellie. How do I choose between them?

Forcing myself to separate what needs to be done and caring for Kellie, I finally consider my options through the eyes of an officer. What would I tell a family member in this same situation? Then, the answer comes to me. Jackson has been standing nearby trying to keep the ever-growing crowd at bay. There's no chance of me leaving Kellie, so I turn to one of the few men I trust with my life for help once more.

"Jackson, I need you to keep searching while I stay here."

"Are you sure?"

"I can't leave her alone. When her parents get here, I'll find you."

He nods and pats my shoulder. "Don't worry, I'll take care of it. Just make sure she's okay."

When Jackson is only a few steps away, Kellie grabs my wrist. "Lance, you have to go with him."

"No, I won't leave you, not right now." As much as I want to be out searching beside Jackson and my family of blue, knowing they are out there doing everything they can to find Rory makes my decision to stay here a little easier to bear.

Out of the corner of my eye, I see the paramedic's approach with a gurney. I realize I recognize both Adam and Sharon from work. I'm relieved as they are two of the best first responders.

"Deputy Malloy, who's this?" Adam asks while setting a medical bag down and kneeling beside me.

"This is my girlfriend, Kellie Bryant. She passed out and hit her head on the concrete." I stand and step back so they can assess her without me being in their way.

"Hey, Kellie, I'm Adam." He pulls a penlight from his shirt pocket and checks her pupils while Sharon slips a blood pressure cuff on her left arm. "Do you feel any pain?"

"No, I need to get up." She pushes Adam's hands away. "My little girl is missing and…" Kellie groans and holds her stomach. "Oh, God, I'm going to be sick." He guides her back down and rolls her onto her side just as she begins to dry heave.

"It feels like I've been kicked in the head." Kellie curls into a ball, pulling her legs up to her chest. Another wave of nausea hits. She covers her mouth with one hand while wrapping an arm protectively around her belly. A sheen of sweat coats her face. It's killing me to see her hurting and knowing I can't do anything to make it better.

"Kellie, it's essential that you are honest with us. On a

scale of one to ten, how bad is your pain?" Adam pats Kellie's arm reassuringly. "I just want to help you get back to your little girl."

"About six or seven." She closes her eyes again then pushes her palms against her temples.

"Alright. I need to get you up and onto the gurney. Do you think you can stand?" Adam asks.

Before Kellie can answer, I lift her into my arms and take a moment to cradle her close to my chest, where I know she's safe. Once she's settled, I pull the blanket up over her legs, then reach for the safety straps to buckle her up.

"How's your pain now?" Sharon asks while digging through her medical bag.

"It's getting worse." Her tears fall freely as she clutches the sides of her head. "Please just make the pain go away so I can keep looking for Rory."

She's in a lot of pain and isn't thinking clearly. I've seen it so many times before. No matter what Kellie tells herself, there's no way she's capable of searching for Rory.

"I'm going to insert an IV which will put some much-needed fluids into you." You'll feel a slight sting." Sharon swipes Kellie's arm with an alcohol wipe and inserts the needle before starting an IV. "Now, let's see what we can do about that pain." She adds more medication to the line then pats Kellie's shoulder. "You should feel better in just a moment."

"Lance, can I talk to you?" Adam leads me away. "Kellie might have a concussion, but it could be worse. We need to get her to the hospital now."

"I agree. I'll call Kellie's parents and have them meet us there." Returning to Kellie's side, I pull out my phone to call her mom but stop when she reaches for my hand.

"Lance, I'm really sleepy." She blinks, struggling to stay awake. "I need to keep looking for Rory."

"Just rest, for now, sweetheart," I speak in a soothing tone while leaning in to kiss her forehead gently. The medication has taken effect quicker than expected, and her eyes are already heavy.

"But I have to find her." She mumbles softly.

"I need you to trust me." Even though she's almost asleep, I need to reassure her that I will find Rory and bring her home.

"I do trust you." Her breathing slows to a steady rhythm, and I know she's fallen into a deep sleep.

I tuck Kellie's hand under the blanket and help push the gurney quickly across the park to where the ambulance is located. The group of people surrounding us earlier are gone, and they've returned to minding their own business.

As we are loading the gurney into the back of the ambulance, I hear Kellie's father, Tom, and turn to see him running toward us. Angie is right behind him. "Lance!"

"What happened?" Angie grabs the metal rail on the gurney while her eyes sweep over her daughter.

"She passed out and hit her head." Seeing the terrified looks on both their faces I add, "They gave her some pain medication and need to get her to the hospital now."

"And what about Rory?" Tom asks while Adam and Sharon finish securing the gurney in the back of the ambulance.

"I'm sorry, we haven't found her yet." As difficult as it is admitting my failure to her father, I can't change the facts and need to push forward. "I don't have time to go over everything right now, but I need you to go with Kellie, so I can concentrate on finding Rory."

"I'll ride with her, Tom. You follow behind in our car." Angie climbs in beside Kellie and buckles the seat belt around her waist. I expected her to break down, but instead, her calm strength shines through.

"Okay. I'll be right behind you." Tom digs into his pocket and retrieves his keys. "Lance, you need to call us immediately with an update about Rory."

He helps me close the heavy doors then runs to his car.

As they drive away, my phone rings. "What is it, Jackson?"

"Lance, man, you need to get over to the path on the east side of the park." His heavy breathing and the distinct jingling of keys on his duty belt tell me he's running.

"Have they found Rory?"

"Not yet, but we have information that might be of help."

"What information?"

"We have a male witness who saw an adult female and child walking near the grove of redwood trees."

"I'm on my way. Don't let him go until I get there."

Sprinting across the park, I notice Jackson talking to a guy I assume is the witness he spoke of moments ago.

Frustrated by the amount of time that has passed since Rory disappeared, I step between them and interrupt. "Are you the one who saw my little girl?"

"Whoa, Lance. Slow down. I got this." Jackson murmurs to me and places his hand on my arm. The guy stares at me with wide eyes. In my desperation for answers, I've grabbed a fistful of his shirt and dragged him toward me. "Let him go, Lance."

Releasing a breath, I do as Jackson orders and step back. "Shit, I'm so sorry."

"No harm. I'd be the same way if my daughter was missing."

"This is Tyler." Jackson introduces him, but I couldn't care less about his name. I just want to know what he saw.

"Did you see the woman that walked away with the girl?"

He nods. "Yeah, but I didn't get a great look at her."

"Can you give us any sort of description of the woman?"

"Not much. She was hot and caught my eye. I've always had a thing for brunettes with long hair, so…"

"How old would you say she is?" Jackson asks. "What was her skin tone like?"

"Light skinned and if I had to guess, she was in her late twenties or early thirties. It's hard to tell nowadays."

"Come on. You must remember more." His absent stare pisses me off. I should be searching, not waiting on information that means nothing. "Just forget it. This is a waste of time."

I catch Jackson's judgmental glare. I shouldn't be pushing Tyler so hard, but frustration has taken hold, forcing me to go against everything I've been taught about interviewing a witness.

"Lance, back off. I'll handle this." He grabs my shoulder, pulling me back. Jackson turns to Tyler. "What about the woman's clothing?"

"Grey sweatpants and a white T-shirt, I think."

I grit my teeth and count to ten. "Come on, Tyler. My little girl is missing. Think hard."

"I'm sorry. I really want to help you find her." He looks up to the sky and scrunches his face up as if searching his memory for more information.

"Forget it. Jackson, we need to keep looking."

"Wait!" Tyler's head snaps up, meeting my gaze. "She was carrying one of those gigantic, overpriced purses my wife keeps asking for. The brown one with the gold initials all over it."

"Hang on." An image flashes in my mind. I know the purse he's talking about because I purchased one as a gift for Trish.

Jackson raises his eyebrow in question but doesn't interrupt.

"If you saw a picture of the lady, do you think you'd recognize her?" Pulling out my phone, I swipe through my old pictures hoping I didn't delete the one I'm looking for.

"Possibly. It's worth trying, I guess." Tyler's lack of confidence is worrying, but I keep searching through my phone, knowing there's a sliver of hope it might help us find who took Rory.

"Got it!" It's a picture of Trish from her birthday party a while back. It's the same day I gave her that expensive designer bag she'd been hinting at for months.

Turning my phone so Tyler can see the screen, I ask, "Could this be the woman you saw?"

"Maybe." He shrugs his shoulders. "Her hair kind of looks the same."

"Here." I expand the picture to focus on Trish's face. "Look again?"

Tyler studies the screen longer this time. "Yeah, yeah. That's definitely her."

Blowing out a breath, I turn my phone so that Jackson can see the picture.

"Holy shit! It was Trish that took her?"

"We need to find Rory now. Who the hell knows what that crazy bitch is planning."

"Thanks, Tyler." Jackson puts his notebook in his pocket. "I have your information if we need to contact you later."

"I'm just glad I could help." Not wanting to waste any more time, I run towards the path Tyler said he last saw Trish and Rory walking down.

"Hurry up!" I call over my shoulder to Jackson.

"Lance, hang on." He catches up to me. "We need a plan."

Out of breath already, I slow down. "Fine, I'll go off to the left, close to the creek, you go to the right. We need to spread out, but since I don't have a radio to contact dispatch, stay within earshot." Adrenaline pumps through me and pushes me into action. *I swear I'll kill Trish if Rory has one scratch on her.*

"Got it. I'll let dispatch know our current position."

It doesn't take long before I'm deep into the wooded area. It's almost impossible to see through the overgrown brush, foliage, and around the giant tree trunks. They must be twenty to thirty feet in diameter. Big enough that Trish could be hiding behind one and I wouldn't know it. "How the hell am I going to see anything?"

The longer Trish is out here with Rory, the less chance there is I'll get her back. I could strangle her for what she's putting Kellie through, but even more for taking Rory in the first place. *Wait! Not if, but when I find Rory. Failure isn't an option and I need to stay positive.* "RORY!" Jackson calls out from nearby.

Pushing aside my fears, I pause and listen for any signs they might be in the immediate vicinity.

"RORY! It's Lance."

Hearing what sounds like someone running and twigs breaking in front of me, I pick up my pace. "Jackson, follow me!"

"Right behind you!"

"Rory. It's Lance." Thorns and branches tear at the exposed skin on my legs. Pushing through a large bush, a branch smacks me in the face, but I keep going.

"Lance, slow down." Jackson comes to a stop. "Listen. I heard something over in those bushes. We need to check it out."

I freeze when I hear Rory's voice and turn my head in the direction the sound came from. "Jackson! Stop! Do you hear that?"

We stand in silence and wait but hear nothing more.

"Damn it. I swear I heard Rory's voice." Maybe my mind wants to hear her so much it's playing tricks on me.

"Try calling for her again."

"Rory, it's Lance. If you can hear me, yell as loud as you can." We both stand perfectly still and wait.

"I don't hear anything. Let's keep—"

"Shh!" I hear her voice again and throw up my hand to silence Jackson.

"Help!" Rory's soft voice cuts through the quiet and stabs my heart.

"Rory! It's Lance. I'm coming." Turning in the direction of her voice, I take off at full speed with Jackson beside me.

Ducking under branches and weaving between trees, my feet get tangled in a patch of vines, causing me to fall flat on my face, knocking the air from my lungs. "Oof."

"Lance!" Rory calls out louder this time.

"Rory. Stay where you are. I'm coming to get you." Ignoring the pain in my ankle, I push up and continue searching.

"She has to be close by," Jackson says, running past me.

"I'm scared." Fear laced in her scream brings both Jackson and me to a sudden halt.

"Don't be afraid. Can you hear me still?" Not sure which direction to go, we turn in a circle and listen for her to answer.

"Yes." Her reply is a soft whimper.

"Rory, I need you to shout as loud as you can. Tell me where you are?" I need to keep her talking.

"I'm hiding." Her yell has a hollow, almost echoey sound like she's in a cave.

"Where could she be hiding?" Jackson grumbles. He pulls at the front of his ballistic vest, adjusting it while walking away to search the surrounding area.

"Can you see anything around you?"

"No, it's dark." Her cries are louder than before. "I want Addy K."

"I know, baby. Just keep talking to me so I can find you."

I turn in a slow circle, scanning carefully for any place she could be hiding

"Lance, over here." I hurry over to where he is standing a few yards away from me. He points to a burned-out giant redwood tree trunk with a cut out near the roots. It's big enough for her to climb into and hide but is too small for either of us to do more than look inside. "I hear her, but she doesn't know me, and I don't want to scare her even more."

"You're right." I look up to the heavens and pray Rory is there.

"Rory? Are you in here?" Lowering myself to my hands and knees, I look inside, but with only a sliver of sunlight shining through the split in the wood, I can't see anything. "It's too dark. Jackson, I need you over here with your flashlight."

Jackson kneels beside me and shines the light into the space. My heart sinks to the pit of my stomach when I see Rory huddled into the back of the hollow tree trunk. Her ponytails are undone and the once pink T-shirt she wears is now smudged with dirt and ash from the charred wood. She's a mess, but all that matters is that we found her.

"Jackson, she's in here." Wanting to shout with joy but not scare Rory, I hold back and speak softly.

"Thank God." Jackson dips his head exhales deeply.

"Rory, honey. It's me, Lance. Can you crawl over to me?" Her eyes are downcast. She's scared, but I need her to know she is safe. "Just a little way and I've got you." I can't push her, not too hard. She moves a little and I'm filled with hope. "Good girl, just a little bit more." She comes close enough for me to touch but stops short in front of the opening. Tenderly,

I lift her chin with my two fingers and catch her bloodshot eyes in mine. It's too much suffering for one so young. Tears fill her eyes and her chin wobbles. I move back to give her space to crawl out. "Sweetheart. A bit closer and I've got you." She's unsure for a moment then lunges into my arms. Her body trembles while she snuggles into the crook of my neck.

"I want Addy K."

"I'll take you right to her, but you're safe now." I continue whispering words of comfort. My hands shake while rubbing circles on her back until her tears subside. "Shh, baby girl. I've got you."

"I was scared."

"It's okay, Rory. I won't let you go." I feel her settle into my arms, but I need to check that she is okay physically. "Does anything hurt?" I pull her away from my chest so I can look her over better.

She points to her scraped and bloody knees. "I fell."

I push down the anger I feel towards Trish. Her time will come, but right now I need to take care of Rory. "Oh, no. Don't worry, I'll take you to Addy K and she will make everything feel better."

"I wanna go home."

As much as I want to ask her questions about who took her and what happened, I know I need to get her out of here and safely into Kellie's arms. "Me too. Let's go find your Addy K, then get you home."

I'd almost forgotten Jackson was there. "Lance, before we go, there's just one thing we need to do." He turns up his radio, allowing me to hear. "Deputy Locke to dispatch." He releases the button on his radio, waiting for a reply.

"Dispatch to Deputy Locke. What is your status?"

"10-8. All clear. Deputy Malloy has the child. She is safe. I'll handle her transport to the hospital."

The dispatcher repeats Jackson's status and cheers erupt over her radio from others in the emergency services office.

"Are you ready to go find Addy K?" She nods and lays her head back on my shoulder.

Staring down at Rory's angelic face, I feel like I could take on the whole world right now to keep her safe. Well, maybe not the whole world, but I'm prepared to deal with Trish.

5

KELLIE

Tilting my chin toward the cloudless sky, I squint as the sun shines on my face. Slowly, I turn in a full circle to scan the area for clues. We've been searching for hours and still, there's been no sign of Rory.

I've separated from the group to continue looking in a part of town I'm not familiar with. In front of me is a black wrought iron fence surrounding an abandoned farmhouse. An uneasy feeling creeps over me while staring at the building that should have been torn down years ago. The possibility of Rory hiding inside is the only motivation I need to look closer.

Choosing my steps carefully, I walk through the tall grass that has taken over the garden area. The tattered curtains fluttering through the broken glass with the slight breeze reminds me of an old horror movie I watched as a kid.

"Addy K, help."

"Rory!" My head snaps up when I hear her crying from inside the house. Her high-pitched scream brings forward a rage I've never felt before. Racing up the three wooden porch stairs, my foot disappears through a rotten plank, causing me to trip and crash to my knees.

"Hurry, I'm scared." She cries out again.

"I'm coming for you!" Scrambling to my feet, I'm in pain from my fall, but nothing will stop me. I try to enter the house, but when I turn the knob, the door doesn't open. Something must be blocking it from the inside. Using my shoulder, I shove with strength I never knew I had.

"Addy K!" Her voice echoes around the empty house, providing no clear direction for me to start searching.

"Tell me where you are." Running from room to room, I frantically fling open doors and check inside closets.

Movement from behind the faded, red velvet curtains that hang from floor to ceiling draws my attention. Whipping back the worn fabric, the iron rod breaks away from the wall, sending it and the curtains crashing down on me.

Cloaked in darkness, I roll side to side, kicking my legs in an attempt to free myself from the fabric. But the more I move around, the more tangled I become. Sweat coats my entire body while I continue to struggle. My lungs burn as I inhale the musty air and tears sting my eyes. Finally, I throw the curtain off my body, just as a blood curdling scream pierces the air.

"No! Don't hurt her!"

"Kellie, calm down." A female voice startles me awake.

"Let me go. I have to find Rory." I lash out wildly, flailing my arms, striking the person pushing down on my shoulders. Breaking free from their hold, I sit up, and my eyes dart around the room.

"Kellie, stop! You're safe." Instantly I recognize my mother's stern voice and quit struggling. "You're in the hospital.

My vision is blurred, and my head feels heavy. Multiple wires are connected to my chest and an IV is inserted into the vein in the back of my hand and taped down. There's an odd ringing in my ears, along with the beeping from the monitors and machines beside my bed.

"Shh, lay back down." She guides me down onto the mattress and pulls the blanket back over my body.

"I was having a nightmare that someone took Rory, and she was inside a house crying." Pain streaks through my skull like a lightning bolt when I speak and my stomach rolls in time with the thundering in my head.

"That explains your screams while you were sleeping." She sweeps my hair off my forehead, tucking it behind my ears. "Can you remember anything from earlier today?"

The thick fog clouding my vision has me feeling disoriented and confused. Looking at her carefully, I see her brow is pulled tight with worry. Her hair is a mess and looks as if she's been raking her fingers through it. Dark smudges under her red-rimmed eyes are in stark contrast to her pale complexion. I've only seen her this distressed on one previous occasion; when I told her that her firstborn daughter, my sister, Leslie, was dead.

I close my eyes, searching for a sliver of recollection, and wonder what could have occurred today that would have her so upset.

"I remember going to the park with Lance and Rory for a picnic." My eyes are closed while I pull those images to the forefront of my mind. "They were feeding each other some fruit." Remembering the two most important people in my life laughing and having fun brings a smile to my face.

"What else?" Mom fidgets with her hands. Her chewed fingernails set off an alarm inside my head.

"Then Rory was playing with her friends while Lance and I were talking…" The words stick in my throat when the next memory comes forward. "No!" A chill runs down my spine, and for a moment, I hold my breath.

Mom opens her mouth to speak, but I cut her off.

I'm trying to hold myself together, but I begin to remember everything. "I thought it was just a nightmare."

Vivid memories return, each one worse than the last. It's as if I'm watching the most terrifying movie and being forced to sit in the theater until the end. Only I'm not sure there will be an ending.

As the events from today become clearer, the monitor beside my bed beeps louder and faster. "The last thing I remember is yelling for Rory and feeling dizzy. Then I was laying down, staring up at Lance, while he begged me to trust him to bring Rory home safe."

"Have they found Rory yet?" Mom picks nervously at her cuticles. A few beads of blood appear, and she dabs at it with an old tissue. "Mom, look what you're doing to your fingers."

"I'm fine, love."

"You're hiding something from me?" She cringes when I shout. Fear of the unknown amps up my anxiety and a cold sweat covers my body. *Please don't let her tell me Rory is hurt, or worse, dead.*

"It's just that they haven't found her yet." Her forehead creases and I see her choosing her words carefully. "And I thought I lost you too." She gathers me into her arms and sobs.

"You didn't lose me." I squeeze her tight and wait for her tears to slow. "And we will find Rory."

Losing Leslie almost killed my mom. She tried to hide her depression and be strong for me, but I saw through her act. I can only imagine how she felt getting the call about Rory being missing and then seeing me passed out on the ground. I'm surprised she's still standing and not lying in a bed next to me.

A soft knock on the door interrupts our moment. "Ms. Bryant, it's good to see that you're awake." The male nurse walks into the room with a broad, friendly smile then presses buttons on the monitors until they are silent. "How are you feeling now?"

"Like I've been run over by a truck, but I'm ready to leave."

"You're not ready to be discharged quite yet, not until we check you over."

I feel like shit, but there's nothing that will keep me here while Rory is missing.

"Kellie, you can't leave. Your head–" Mom challenges me, but the nurse cuts her off.

"Okay, sweetie," he dismisses me with a soft pat on my hand. "Let's wait and see what the doctor has to say. He should be here in just a bit. Lay back down and I'll go and find him." He pushes another button a few times and the beeping returns but at a much slower rate.

"What is the big machine I'm hooked to?" Warmth flows through my veins and my body feels heavy.

"The doctor has you on a pain relief drip." He grins at me, but I don't return the gesture. Having painkillers running through me will no doubt delay my release. "Once the doctor comes in, he'll explain more." He turns on his heel and I hear the squeak from his ugly rubber clogs as he walks down the hall.

As frustrated as I am about the medication, I can appreciate the relief from the constant pounding in my head.

Trying to stay awake, I ask, "Where's Dad?"

"He went back to the park to help with the search."

"So, what do we do now?" I lay back on the pillow. "I feel useless just laying here."

"Lance said he will find her." Mom takes my hand but turns her face away from me, no doubt trying to hide her emotions. Tears fall freely down her cheeks before she can wipe them away. "We have to have faith."

"So, we just wait?"

"And pray." I've never known her to be the religious type,

but I follow her lead and lower my head offering my own plea to the universe to make this nightmare go away.

Mom and I stay silent with just the slow beeping of the heart monitor and the low murmur of voices coming from the corridor. Within minutes, she gives in to her exhaustion and falls asleep in the chair beside me. The turmoil of the past year with Leslie's death and today's events seems to have taken its toll. Even in slumber, I can see the wrinkles around her eyes are more profound than I remember. Mom's shoulder length hair is slowly turning from a deep auburn to a beautiful silver, just like my grandmother's.

My heart wars between wanting to leave the hospital to search and doing as I am told.

Staring at the large clock on the wall, I count the minutes, eager for the doctor to arrive. Each full rotation of the second hand seems to take longer, pulling me into a trance. The time between my blinks increases and I finally surrender to my body's need for sleep.

A loud commotion startles me awake. My eyes snap open when I hear shouting and running footsteps from the corridor. A quick glance at the clock tells me it's only been fifteen minutes since I last noted the time.

"Mom? What's all that noise?"

"I don't know. I must have fallen asleep." She rubs her eyes then walks to the door, opening it just enough to peer through the crack.

"Oh, thank God!" She shrieks and pulls the door open completely.

"Sir, you need to check in at the emergency department." I recognize my nurse's voice.

"I'm going to call security." Another female voice calls out.

"Look, you do whatever you need to do. Follow me if you want, but I'm bringing this little girl to her aunt right now. Now tell me where Kellie Bryant's room is?"

Mom steps into the hallway and waves her hands excitedly. "Lance! Hurry! Kellie's in here."

Before I can sit up, Lance is standing in the doorway holding Rory on his hip like he always does. It takes every ounce of willpower I have to not rip the IV out and run to them.

Rory smiles brightly, seemingly unaffected by everything that's happened today. She has a red lollipop in one hand and a juice box in the other. Her T-shirt is filthy, and hair is a gnarled mess, but to my eyes, she looked perfect.

Lance's clothes are also dirty and disheveled. "Look who's here?" His forced smile doesn't hide the tension in his jaw or the tears welling up in his eyes.

My body trembles with an overload of emotions. Stunned into silence, I can't do anything but reach out for my niece. All I want to do is hold her close and never let her go again.

Lance places Rory into my open arms and backs away.

"Addy K, Lance found me." She looks at me then turns her sweet smile on Lance. He's her hero in every sense of the word.

"Yes, baby. He did find you." Clutching her close to my chest, I pepper her with kisses and thank God she's safe. Not wanting to upset her, I bite down on my lip to keep the tears at bay.

"I'm so sorry, Kellie. I tried to call both you and your Mom's cell phones but couldn't get through."

"It's fine. All that matters is she's here now." My focus returns to Rory as she protests my hold on her.

"Addy K, you're squishing me." She wiggles in an attempt to free herself, but I keep my arms wrapped protectively around her, just not as tight this time.

Rory pulls back and points to the bandage on my head. "Do you have a boo-boo?"

"A little one, but I'll be okay. But it looks like you scraped your knees."

She nods, "Yep, I need band-aids."

I kiss the tips of my fingers and touch them gently to each knee. "Do they feel a little better now?"

"Yes, but I still want band-aids." Her lopsided grin melts my heart and changes the mood of the room in an instant.

"Of course you do," I chuckle.

It's no surprise when she copies me by kissing my forehead. "All better now?"

"Yes. Much better." Pulling her into another hug, I thank God for bringing her back to me unharmed. "You always make everything better."

Completely lost in this special moment, I forgot about everyone else in the room. Mom, Dad, Lance, and a few hospital staff have been watching our reunion, and not one of them has a dry eye.

As the staff members quietly file out of the room, my nurse from earlier slips out the door, closing it behind him.

Mom sniffles and comes to stand beside us, kissing Rory's cheek and then mine.

"Hi, Gram Gram." She drinks the remainder of her juice with a loud slurp.

"Hey, little one." Mom takes the empty juice box from her hand.

"Where's Grumpa?" Rory asks with a tilt of her head.

"I'm right here, kiddo."

"Grumpa! Rory wiggles her way loose of my hold, then slides down the bed and jumps into his arms. As much as I hate to let her go, I know my parents need time to hold her too. Processing all that has happened will take a long time for all of us, except Rory it seems.

"Knock, knock." Rory's pediatrician peeks his head in the room. "I was already here for another patient and heard the nurses talking about Rory's little adventure today. I told the ER doctor I'd come to check on her."

"Look, Rory. It's Dr. Michaelson." She gives a little wave then snuggles back into Grumpa's chest.

Although she seems fine, I know she needs to be examined, and I'm grateful he's the doctor to do it.

"Hi, Rory. How about you come with me for a bit? We can find nurse Gloria so she can listen to your heartbeat."

"But I want to stay with Addy K," she whines and reaches out for me. Even though I know I shouldn't, everything inside me says to give her exactly what she wants.

Before I can protest, my father runs interference. As if knowing my fears, he looks to me first. "How about Gram Gram and I go with her?" I nod, then he turns his attention to Rory. "Then we can get some chocolate ice cream."

Dad has always been able to talk her into anything. Or maybe it's just his legendary bribery skills. Either way, she takes no time at all to agree with him, under her terms, of course. "Okay, but I want strawberry ice cream."

"Strawberry it is," Dr. Michaelson agrees and leads them out the door, leaving Lance and me behind.

An awkward silence lays heavy between us. There's so much we need to talk about. Where did he find Rory? Does he know what happened or who took her? Not to mention my need to apologize and hope he can forgive me for how I acted.

I struggle for the right words to say, unsure if any of it will make up for how terrible I treated him. Finally, I decide to just blurt it out.

"I'm sorry." Shame and regret engulf me now that Rory is no longer in danger. "I said some really horrible things today that I wish I could take back."

"You have nothing to be sorry for. Today was a disaster, but thankfully, Rory is safe, and that's all that matters now."

"But the things I said to you were awful."

"I won't pretend it didn't hurt, but in the heat of the moment, things are often said that we don't mean."

"I didn't mean them. I was just so scared we'd never see Rory again and took it out on you." I reach for his hand, relieved when he takes it in his. "In reality, I was angry at myself."

"I know you didn't mean them." He kisses me gently on the lips. "Besides, you can't get rid of me that easily."

"Ouch." A sharp pain hits from behind my eyes, and my vision becomes blurry again. Laying back on the pillow, I grimace with each pulse in my temple.

"What's wrong?"

"It's my head. It still hurts." I squeeze my eyes closed tight. "Can you turn off the lights?"

He clicks a few buttons, and the room dims. "Is that better?"

Opening one eye at a time, I allow them to adjust and refocus. "Much better, thank you."

"I'll go find the doctor and see if he can check on you before Rory comes back."

"Okay, I'm just going to rest my eyes a bit."

"Kellie, honey, wake up. The doctor is here." Lance strokes my cheek and I lean into his touch. Opening my eyes slowly, I'm grateful the lights are still off.

"Where's Rory? How long was I asleep?"

"She's still with your parents." His eyes flick to the clock. "You've been asleep for about an hour."

"Ms. Bryant, I'm Dr. Gerard. How are you feeling?"

"Great if you've got a twin brother standing next to you. If not, I must be in pretty bad shape since I can see two of you." I chuckle and regret it as the sound ricochets around my skull.

"Not a twin, so the double vision is a problem. I'm keeping you overnight so that we can monitor you."

"No, I can't stay, I have to take care of Rory."

"Before you protest too much, we've already made plans for another bed to be brought up to your room so Rory can stay with you. How does that sound?"

Lance is grinning and I get the feeling he's pre-empted my extended stay and is behind this unusual arrangement, though I'm still not happy I won't be going home to my own bed.

"Thank you. I think that will work just fine."

"Rory is a wonderful little girl. She's captured the hearts of the entire staff who are excited to dote on her some more."

"I'm not surprised. She has that one wrapped around her little finger." I gesture with my thumb towards Lance.

"She sure does," Lance says without a trace of embarrassment.

"Well, now that the sleeping arrangements are covered, there is something else I need to discuss with you." He looks to Lance then back to me. "Privately."

"Uh, okay. Lance, can you go find out what's taking so long with Rory?"

"Yeah, sure." I sense his reluctance, but he kisses my cheek and steps out the door.

Dr. Gerard closes my chart and pulls a chair over beside the bed.

"We ran multiple tests when you first came in. Some routine and others specific to your head injury." He rubs his finger on his chin. "Along with your concussion, the results showed something interesting."

"What do you mean by interesting?" This can't be good. I sit up too fast and grasp the sides of my head. "You're freaking me out a little. Can you please just tell me what you're talking about?"

"It's nothing bad, I promise. Let's start with you telling me when you had your last period?"

"I really have no idea. But why would you need to know that for a concussion?"

He cocks his head to the side with a silly grin then it hits me.

"Wait, am I pregnant?"

"Yes!"

"Are you sure?" My hands instantly wrap protectively around my belly. I can't believe this is happening. I've been on the same birth control pills since I was sixteen.

"Well, the test results generally don't lie. 99% of the time, they are accurate, but there is that 1% and the reason I've scheduled an ultrasound."

"Um...when will they do the test?"

"The nurse will be here shortly to take you to radiology."

"Alright, thank you," I reply softly, still trying to absorb his words as he walks out the door.

The swing of emotions from complete devastation to utter joy has my head spinning and all the bad has disappeared. Thinking back to the conversation Lance and I were having right before everything turned to shit, I wonder if he's ready for his life to change forever.

Returning to my room after the ultrasound, I stare at the black and white picture. The scratchy image is mostly black with a tiny peanut-sized circle.

The sonographer's words play on a loop in my mind. "Congratulations, Ms. Bryant, you're going to be a mommy again, and Rory is going to be a big sister."

I was still in shock when the obstetrician came to my room and briefly explained the risks to the baby due to my concussion. When I asked about the painkillers and how they might affect the baby, she assured me that none of the medications they've given me should cause any complications with my pregnancy, but I can't help but worry. She set an appointment for me to see her next week and suggested I make a list of questions for when I see my personal doctor.

"This has been one crazy day." Rubbing my still flat belly, I imagine what it will be like once the baby grows and stretches my skin to the size of a watermelon. "I can do this. Ready or not, this little one is coming."

"Guess who's back?" Lance calls from behind the slightly ajar door.

"Is it Santa Claus?"

"Nope. Guess again."

"Ummmm, the man in the moon?"

"It's me!" Rory rushes into the room with a bouquet of balloons trailing behind her. Lance follows her inside with his arms loaded with stuffed animals and a huge vase with several dozen red roses.

"Who were you talking to?" Lance looks around the room, confusion written on his face.

"No one, just mumbling to myself."

"Gotcha." He unloads the toys on the small pull-out sofa and places the vase on the table beside me. "These are for you."

"The stuffed animals are mine, but Lance said the balloons are for us to share." Rory hands me the balloon strings and runs over to the sofa to play. I'm still floored by how she's bounced back into the same happy little girl from this morning.

"Where did all of these gifts come from?"

"This is only the tip of the iceberg. There's a lot more coming."

On cue, three hospital volunteers enter the room, pushing carts loaded with flowers and assorted presents.

"You've got to be kidding me? This is too much." I watch in awe as a nurse sets a fruit basket beside the roses.

"You're a part of our family of blue now."

"So, wait a minute. All this stuff is from people you work with?"

"Yeah, and some are from other agencies and fellow officers I don't know. When an incident like today occurs involving a member of the law enforcement community, we rally around each other."

"I'm overwhelmed. I've never seen anything like this before."

"Get used to it. We celebrate big in this family."

His chest puffs up. I haven't seen this level of confidence and pride in him ever. It looks good on him.

"Lance, will you help me put my new friends on my bed?" Rory asks, tugging him over to where she wants him to be.

"Of course. Who should we start with?"

Watching them plan where to place each animal before setting up her bed for the night, I consider how different life will be with the little one growing inside me. If this family of blue has huge celebrations, I imagine Lance planning a colossal gala when I tell him about the baby. At least I hope he'll be that excited to learn he's going to be a daddy.

6

LANCE

"Dinner's here." I hold up two large plastic bags filled with burgers and fries from Helen's diner.

"Thank God! I'm starving." Kellie pulls the hospital table toward her, and I hand her the Styrofoam takeout box.

"I'm starving too." Rory bounces on her toes impatiently. She's been snacking all day on sugary treats, so I'll be shocked if she eats any dinner.

"Go sit with Grandma and I'll bring it to you." Rory scurries over and squeezes herself between Angie and Tom on the tiny sofa.

"This is so much better than what the hospital tried passing off as macaroni and cheese." Kellie takes a big bite of her cheeseburger and sips from her cup of sweet tea.

"I agree. That plate of orange goo looked worse than the box of instant mashed potatoes your mom tried feeding us when you and Leslie were Rory's age." Tom teases and reaches for his burger and fries.

"Hey, I had a two-for-one coupon and thought it was worth trying." Angie slaps her husband's arm playfully, then turns her attention back to Rory, who's quietly eating and watching cartoons on her *iPad*.

"As wallpaper paste maybe." Tom leans over Rory and places a kiss on Angie's cheek. The emotional ups and downs of the day are slowly slipping away for Kellie and her parents, but I'm still on high alert. My instincts tell me Trish isn't done yet, but I won't let her get close to them again.

"Thanks for having dinner delivered." Kellie dips a fry into a small plastic cup of mustard and pops it into her mouth.

"No problem. I'm glad to see you eating something." I didn't realize how hungry I was until the delicious aroma from the food hit me. Grease dribbles down my chin after taking a large bite of my double cheeseburger. It's exactly the way a good burger should be.

"I'm stuffed already." Kellie closes the lid but not before I see she has only taken a few bites.

"But you barely ate anything." Kellie's shift from ravenous to full, after eating very little, has me worried. "I'll go get the doctor."

"No! Wait! I don't need to see the doctor." Kellie stops me before I can open the door. "I'm fine. It's been a long day and I'm starting to get sleepy. I'll save the rest of my burger for when I get hungry again later."

Kellie won't look me in the eyes. There's definitely something going on, but I'll wait until her parents leave to voice my concerns.

"Well, now, if you can't finish your dinner, there will be no dessert for you tonight." I point at Kellie and shake my finger in mock disapproval.

"I want dessert," Rory doesn't take her eyes off the *iPad*. She's one smart cookie. Even when I think she's not paying attention, she is completely aware of what everyone says.

"Of course you do." Kellie lets out a full-on belly laugh and it's the most beautiful sound I've heard all day.

Just as I take another messy bite, my phone rings in my back pocket. "Shoot. Are there any napkins?" Kellie tosses me a small towel to wipe my hands before pulling out my phone.

"Hello?" I answer without looking at the screen.

"Hey, Lance. How are Kellie and Rory doing?" It's Jackson. I've been expecting his call and debate whether I should stay in the room or move into the hall.

"They're good." All eyes have focused on me. "Umm, give me a second." Not knowing what Jackson has to say, I figure it's best for me to finish this call where Kellie and her parents can't hear my side of the conversation. "It's Jackson. I'll be right back."

Closing the door behind me, I bring the phone back to my ear, and I walk down the busy corridor to a small sitting area. "Sorry, I was in Kellie's room and wanted to talk freely without them hearing. Do you have any updates?"

"Not much, but Lieutenant Cartwright told me to call. He wants to see you right away."

"If there's nothing to report, can't he wait until tomorrow." I'm conflicted. Part of me wants to be at the station going over every detail, but a larger part wants to stay close to Kellie and Rory. I'll be told to keep my distance at some point, and this could be my last chance to get information about the case.

"Look, I'm just the messenger. If Cartwright wants to see you then you damn well better get your ass down here." My pulse quickens when I hear the frustration in Jackson's voice. Momentarily I wonder what has him so riled up. "And the D.A. wants our reports on her desk first thing in the morning."

"Alright, I'll be there as soon as I can." I disconnect the call and shove the phone back into my pocket. There must be more than he's telling me, but the only way I'll get it out of him is a face-to-face meeting.

When I re-enter Kellie's room, I see Rory tucked into bed, surrounded by all of her new stuffed toys. Angie is reading her a story and Tom is watching a ball game on the wall mounted TV.

"What did Jackson want?" Kellie sits forward on the bed.

"Lieutenant Cartwright wants to see me." I toss the rest of my burger in the trash and clean up the condiments and napkins on the small table beside Kellie. "It shouldn't take too long."

"Lance," Kellie whispers and grabs my wrist. "I want to know what's going on. I've tried to be patient, but you haven't told me anything."

"That's because there hasn't been much to tell you and why I need to go. Hopefully, I can get an update before I come back." I've been intentionally vague when Kellie and her parents have asked questions. Until I have the full details from the preliminary investigation, I'll keep my suspicions close to my vest. "As soon as I finish, I'll be back." I kiss her cheek then walk around to tell Rory good night.

"Night night, sweetheart." I brush her bangs away and kiss her forehead.

"Good night," Angie says and continues reading to Rory.

"Tom, can you stay here until I get back?"

"Of course."

"Thanks." I slip out the door before Kellie has a chance to ask more questions.

Walking through the hospital's sliding doors toward the parking lot, I draw the cold night air into my lungs. With each exhale, the tension in my muscles lessens, and I relax a bit more.

The lot is full, and it dawns on me that I have no idea where my truck is parked. Jackson took my keys and had

Javier drop it off a few hours ago. Using my key fob, I set off the alarm, see the flashing headlights, and hear the horn blare from three lanes to my left.

The drive to meet Jackson is short, only fifteen minutes from the hospital, and provides enough time to check in again with my parents. After my initial call to tell them Rory was found and that I was taking her to the hospital, I switched to texting with updates. Even though my last text said I'd call if there were any changes, Mom has been blowing up my phone for the past hour.

I push the button on my steering wheel, activating the hands-free function. "Call Mom."

She answers after the second ring. "It's about time. I've been worried sick." The slight echo and hum in the background indicates she has me on speakerphone.

"I'm sorry to worry you. Everything has been happening so fast, this has been my first chance to call you."

"I understand. That's why we figured we would just come to you."

"What?"

"We should be at your house in about thirty minutes."

"Wait. You're coming here? Now?" I should have known she wouldn't stay away, but I wasn't expecting a visit this late at night.

"Of course we are, Lance. Our granddaughter and daughter-in-law are in the hospital. Nothing would keep us from being there."

"I'm glad you're both coming. Rory will be thrilled to see you and Dad, but..." My knuckles turn white as I squeeze the steering wheel while trying to dial back my irritation. "...it may not seem like a big deal, but please stop referring to Kellie as your daughter-in-law until I can make it official."

"But why?" Mom asks.

"I'm not even sure she's ready to take that step yet."

"I see how you two look at each other. You are meant to be together."

"I hope you're right, but let's focus on one thing at a time. Right now, I need to concentrate on what happened today."

"Fine," she huffs. "I won't mention it again."

"Don't believe her," Dad says loud enough for me to hear.

"I really appreciate you coming to help, but you need to promise me you won't bring up anything about marriage." There's silence, and for a minute, I think the call is lost. "Are you still there?"

"She's pouting," Dad replies, his tone laced with humor.

Only he could get away with such an accusation, especially during this stressful time. I roll my eyes because I've heard this back and forth between them thousands of times and it always leads back to the same thing–true love.

"I am not." I picture her sitting in the passenger seat with her arms crossed, glaring at my father while he tries not to crack a smile.

"If you could see her face right now, she looks like she's sucking on a lemon." I hold back the laughter threatening to erupt but realize it's only decades of marriage and friendship that has afforded him the opportunities to needle her and live to tell the tale.

"Your father thinks he's a comedian." I know she wants to laugh but won't give him the satisfaction.

"He's just teasing, Mom."

"I know," she replies.

"But if you don't mind, can we get back to Kellie?"

"Alright, you win," she huffs, though I know she's not really annoyed. "I promise, no referring to her as my daughter-in-law or talk of marriage, but can I at least still claim Rory as my Granddaughter?"

"Yes, you can still refer to Rory as your granddaughter. I know how much she loves having two sets of grandparents who are so devoted to her." I tend to think the same as my Dad and don't believe she will be able to keep it to herself for long, but I'll take this little victory. Mom would go nuts if she knew how close I came to proposing before Rory disappeared. When Kellie spoke of having more children, the words sat on the tip of my tongue, but we were interrupted by the bells from the ice cream cart.

"Good, because I bought a new T-shirt that says, My Favorite *Disney* Princess Is My Granddaughter, and I can't return it." Mom loves her T-shirts with cute sayings on the front. I can hear the excitement in her voice and don't have the heart to tell her Rory is over princesses. She is currently obsessed with some cartoon police dog on one of those kid's channels.

"Thanks, Mom. I'm sure she'll love it. You spoil her."

"It's what Grandma's do. Now, tell me how Kellie and Rory are doing? Are they home yet?"

"Rory is doing great. You'd never know she was lost for several hours." She still thinks Rory just wandered off. Now isn't the right time to tell the truth.

"Children can be very resilient like that. What scares us is just another adventure for them. And what about Kellie?"

"The doctor is keeping her overnight for observation. I was able to convince him to bring a bed into her room for Rory. I'm not sure she would have agreed otherwise."

"I don't blame her at all. Are you still at the hospital?"

"No, I'm driving to the station to help Jackson with some reports. When I finish, I plan to go back and check in on them."

"Okay then. What do you need us to do for you?"

"Nothing right now, but I'll need help keeping an eye on Kellie and Rory while I'm working."

"Why?" Dad asks.

"I can't go into it right now, but once I have more details, I'll share what I can."

"No problem. We can stay as long as you need us." He doesn't pry, but I'm confident that even though he's a retired officer, he's picked up on my not-so-subtle comments and will ask more questions later.

"Thanks. That puts my mind at ease more than you know. I'm pulling into the station parking lot now. If it's not too late, I'll call you when I leave."

"It's never too late to call your parents."

"Alright, I promise to let you know when I finish." I put the truck in park and turn off the engine. "I love you both."

"We love you too."

Disconnecting the call, I sit in the truck for a few minutes, taking in the silence while I try to clear my head. We still have a lot to do to prove Trish had a hand in Rory's disappearance. It's important we get everything filed in the time allotted and get the smallest of details right before presenting it to the District Attorney.

Jackson agreed to wait until Kellie returns home to take her statement. Rory's will be the most important one and yet the trickiest. The word of a young child is often unreliable in the eyes of the law. Without concrete evidence of Trish's involvement, the District Attorney may not be able to charge her at all. There is no way in hell I'll let that happen. I will make sure Trish is held accountable for her actions one way or another.

Pushing open the large glass doors to the Sheriff's Department lobby, my co-workers rush forward with hugs and pats on the back. Their support is invaluable, and I consider myself lucky to have them on my side.

"I can never thank you enough for all you've done for them." Balloons, flowers, and toys fill every open space in the private hospital room. The number of stuffed animals reminds me of when I visited New York City's renowned FAO Schwartz toy store. "I'm still trying to figure out how I'm going to fit it all into my truck when they come home tomorrow."

There's a collective laugh and a few offers of help before everyone goes back to work.

Walking down the hall toward Lieutenant Cartwright's office, I try to figure out what is so important that it couldn't wait until tomorrow. I stop mid-stride when I see him in the breakroom.

"Hey, Lt. You wanted to talk to me?"

"Lance. Yes, thanks for coming so quickly. Let's go to my office and we can talk there." He motions for me to follow him.

After sitting behind the old metal desk, he removes his glasses and chews on the arm. I've noticed he does this when he has to have a difficult conversation with one of his officers.

"You've been to hell and back today." I suspect he's trying to gauge my mental state. "I heard you say Kellie and Rory are doing well, but what about you?"

"You don't have to worry about me." I avoid the question because I don't have a good answer. One minute I'm fine, then next, I'm ready to find Trish and rip her to shreds. If he's asking if I can handle the stress, well, that remains to be seen.

"That's not an answer."

"You're right, but it's the only one you're going to get right now." My tone borders on insubordination, but he doesn't flinch.

Waiting for his response, I sit back in the chair and look around the room. I've never paid attention to the multiple plaques and awards hanging on the walls before now. Directly behind him is a crayon drawing with three stick figures, holding hands with huge smiles. I assume it was created by his only daughter, Hannah, when she was a child. It sort of reminds me of the many masterpieces Rory has given me since she entered preschool.

"Did Hannah draw that picture?" I'm genuinely interested, but I hope it serves as a distraction as well. I'm not up to talking about my feelings or how I'm going to handle them while this investigation continues. I may not be directly involved, but I will do everything I can to prove Trish is responsible for taking Rory and see that she is prosecuted for kidnapping plus any other charges I can add on as enhancements.

He spins his chair around to look at the picture. "Yeah, she drew that on her first day of kindergarten." I recognize the look of pride as a crooked smile spreads slowly across his face. "It's hard to believe she'll be twenty-one this year."

"Twenty-one? Wow, I guess what they say about kids growing up fast is true."

"Yep. It seems like just yesterday I was taking her to Girl Scouts and weekend soccer tournaments." He turns a picture around on his desk for me to see. It's Hannah all grown up in her high school cap and gown. "Just you wait. You'll find out for yourself just how quickly time flies with Rory."

"I can't even imagine what she'll be like as a teenager, let alone an adult," I mumble to myself and chew on my bottom lip while I consider his words carefully. There's so much I never thought about beyond Rory's childhood. Thinking about her growing up scares the hell out of me. "Oh, hell no!" A low growl crawls up my throat when I think about her growing up and someday being around teenage boys. "She's never dating."

"I said the same thing twenty-one years ago. By the way, it doesn't work." He chuckles and I realize I said that part out loud. "Let's get down to business so you can get back to the hospital. First, I need you to write a supplemental report. Then, after Sergeant Williams approves it, you need to stay away from the investigation."

"But–"

"No buts. I want this case to be ironclad."

"You can't expect me to just sit back and wait for Trish to plan her next move. What would you do if it was Hannah?"

"If it was my daughter, I'd like to think I would trust the police to do their job."

Bullshit! I want to shout, but instead I grit my teeth to keep from lashing out.

"Lance, you don't have to like it, but you know I'm right. Don't do anything stupid that will fuck up this case."

I open my mouth to argue my case further but decide fighting with him will only cause more problems for me in the future. "Yes, Sir." Staying out of the way while everyone else works the case will test my resolve but right now, what choice do I have. "Am I dismissed?"

"Yes. Jackson is waiting in the conference room for you." I stand to leave, but he stops me. "I know this isn't easy for you or Kellie. We all want the same thing and that is to find the person responsible and make a clean arrest that will stick in court and result in a conviction, do you hear me?"

"Yes, Sir." I push my chair back and walk slowly down the hall. *We all want the same thing.* That's not entirely true. Given the opportunity, I'd take a pound of flesh from that bitch and have no regrets doing it.

Turning the corner to enter the conference room, I see Jackson staring intently at his laptop.

"Jackson, have you found anything that will link Trish?" I take the seat beside him and look at an image on the screen of what looks to be a late model Honda.

"Not sure." He turns his laptop so I can see the screen better. "We were called to a neighborhood close to the park about this abandoned car." Jackson eyes me cautiously then scrolls to the next image that shows front end damage. "After running the plates, we found out that it was involved in an accident a month ago, but according to the owner, it was still drivable. The insurance didn't want to pay so they totaled it and had it towed to the junkyard."

"Okay, I'm assuming you have more, or you wouldn't be telling me any of this."

"I'm getting there." He scrolls past several more images of the car and stops on one that knocks the air from my lungs. A black duffle bag, rope, duct tape, and a blue tarp. "These were found in the trunk of that same car."

"I'll fucking kill her." My blood boils and I pound my fist on the table. Each of these items are commonly found in kidnapping cases. "If I get my hands on her, I swear I'll–"

"Lance! You need to watch your mouth." Jackson barks and I snap my eyes up to look directly into his. "If you can't keep your shit together, I'll bounce your ass out of here right now."

"Just tell me how you would react if you were me?" I hold up my hand before he can reply. "And don't fucking bother giving me the politically correct answer!" My chest heaves and for the first time in my life, I understand the frustration a victim feels when we placate them about their concerns. "You'd be acting exactly the same way I am now. You would do everything in your power to protect your family."

"Deputy Malloy." My voice must have been louder than I intended and has drawn the unwanted attention of Captain Sheridan. He's standing in the doorway glaring at me. "Is there a problem that I need to deal with?"

Shit. I'll be lucky to get any more information now that the Captain knows I'm here.

"No, no problem at all, Sir." I focus my gaze on Jackson, daring him to disagree with me.

"No, Sir. I've got everything under control." Although glad Jackson agreed with me, his response pisses me off.

"Good, let's keep it that way." The Captain pins me with his steely eyes then returns to his office across the hall.

"You don't need to control me, Jackson." I clench my fists to push down my anger and prove my point that I can keep a tight rein on my emotions. "I just want to be kept in the loop so I can protect my family."

"Look, I get it. You're understandably angry and I can see you're wiped out after everything that has happened. But you're thinking like an overprotective father, and while it's not a bad thing, it's not going to help us catch whoever took Rory." He closes his laptop and puts it into the carrying case, effectively ending our conversation.

"Don't bullshit me. We both know it was Trish. You can label her however you want around others, but don't play games when it's just us."

"Fine, I'm not going to argue with you right now. Once you get your head on straight, you'll see I'm trying to follow procedures, and you'll be glad I did."

"I know I will, but that doesn't help me right now." I give up the fight and decide to lay my feelings on the line. "The problem is, I'm a cop and I can't just sit around and wait for something bad to happen. Tell me what I can do to help."

"The best thing you can do is trust me. Go back to the hospital and be with your family because they need you and it's no secret that you need them too."

After a lot of convincing, I finally agreed to leave the station and write my report tomorrow. Jackson will take Kellie's statement once she's settled back at home. Knowing he will need to question Rory already has me on edge. Right now, she seems unaffected, but after talking to her doctor, he said the chances of her having a delayed reaction are high. He suggested we watch how she handles her day-to-day activities. Make sure she's sleeping and eating normally. Playing with other kids, that sort of thing. If she seems extra clingy, that can be a sign something is bothering her.

The corridor leading to Kellie's room is almost deserted. I'd called her parents earlier to let them know I was on my way back and that I'd be staying the night. Visiting hours are over, but potential dangers associated with Rory's kidnapping attempt, it was either me or a uniformed officer. The hospital staff agreed my presence was the better option.

When I turn the corner, I'm surprised to see Kellie's father, Tom, is standing outside the door. I pick up my pace, worried that something is wrong.

"Why are you out here? Is everything okay?" Panic has my heart racing. I should have trusted my instincts and stayed with them.

"Slow down. Kellie's asleep and Angie is laying down with Rory. I was waiting for you, hoping we could speak privately."

"Yeah, sure." I glance to the closed door desperate to check on them myself.

"I promise you, they're fine. Now, let's go talk over here." He points to a small sitting area with four chairs and a tv mounted on the wall. "I have a few questions before I let you in to see them."

"What do you mean by let me in?" I'm guessing this is the moment where he tears into me for my mistakes. I've been waiting for his protective side to kick in and I'll accept everything he has to give. But he won't tell me I can't see Kellie, or Rory. I promised to stay by her side, and I won't let her father, or anyone push me away.

"There's no sense pussyfooting around this. While Rory

and I were getting ice cream, she told me someone named Auntie Trish took her." His lips purse into a thin line. "If I remember correctly, Trish is your ex-girlfriend's name, right?"

"It is and she's the primary suspect. My partner is heading up the investigation and will be over tomorrow to take a statement from Kellie and Rory." I run my hand roughly over the stubble covering my chin. "I wasn't trying to keep it from you, but I need to be careful about making any public accusations until we know more. We need more than Rory's statement to confirm the kidnapper."

"Do you believe it was your ex?"

"Between us, yes, I know she's been behind everything. The vandalism to Kellie's car and now today. But I can't prove it."

Tom is quiet. He's sizing me up, trying to figure out if I'm good enough for his daughter. I know I have my faults, but Kellie is mine, and if he doesn't see it now, he will very soon.

"I'll make this simple for you. If this woman is crazy enough to attempt to kidnap my granddaughter, what makes you think you can protect either of them from her in the future?"

"I wish I could guarantee you that nothing bad will ever happen, but life isn't that easy. What I can promise you is that I will do everything in my power, including laying down my life for both of them."

"That's all I needed to hear. I'm trusting you, son." He pats my arm. "Those girls and my wife are all I have left to live for in this world." He takes a moment, and I can guess what's running through his mind. "When Leslie died, a piece of me did too." Another pause is followed by a deep breath. "I most certainly did not do everything I should have done as a father to protect her, but I will not make that same mistake twice."

"Thank you, I know I've screwed up, but there's no way I'll let my guard down again."

"You didn't screw up. There's no way you could have predicted your ex-girlfriend would take Rory. It's not easy being a parent and perfection is a myth. You'll make more mistakes. Hell, I made my own with Leslie, and look what happened. I didn't get a second chance to protect her. Just promise me you'll use this experience and learn from it."

"I will." I swallow hard and take a leap of faith, expecting to be shot down without a second thought. "The day I saw your daughter clutching Rory to her chest changed my life forever. In the chaos surrounding her, Kellie's strength was apparent then and even more so now. She is the most beautiful, intelligent, and loving woman a man could ever dream of meeting. Having her by my side while I buried my best friend was the only thing that got me through the lowest point in my life." I swipe my sweaty palms across my pants. "I love Kellie and Rory and can't imagine a day without them in my life."

"I know you do. I see it every time you look at them and I can see their love for you as well."

"I hope you're right because someday soon, I plan to ask Kellie to be my wife, and I'd like to have your blessing. Not just to marry Kellie, but also to be the father Rory deserves."

7

KELLIE

Sitting beside Lance in the front seat of his truck while driving home from the hospital, I soak up the sun's rays shining through the windshield. With the window open, I rest my arm on the door and enjoy the slight breeze drifting through the cab.

Never in a million years could I have imagined the direction my life has taken or that my happiness would revolve around my niece and the handsome man sitting beside me. It's strange to think how different all of our lives would be right now had Leslie not overdosed less than a year ago.

Unable to sleep last night, I asked myself the hard questions I wasn't sure I was ready to accept the answers to.

What would life be like if Leslie was still with us?

Would I have met Lance?

Would Rory be as happy and healthy as she is right now?

Pain and sorrow coursed through me when I admitted the answer to those questions was a resounding no.

If Leslie had lived, I fear there would have been more heartache and death. The likelihood of Rory thriving, let alone surviving in the environment I found her in, was slim at best. History is known to repeat itself in the life of addiction. Children learn from their parents, and unfortunately, the lessons Rory would have learned most definitely would have led her down the same dead-end path as her mom. Although my thoughts are reprehensible, I can't help but believe my sister's death opened doors for Rory to live a happy, healthy, normal life.

On a deep sigh, I sink back into the seat, close my eyes, and allow the music from the radio to push away the flashbacks that are threatening to ruin my day. There's only one thing I want playing on repeat right now. *Rory is home and safe.*

"Hey, babe. Wake up." Lance rubs my arm. "Your phone is buzzing."

"Shoot, I must have dozed off." Reaching into my bag, I remove my phone and see a text from my mom asking what's taking us so long. I blink the sleep from my eyes and type out a quick message letting her know we'll be home soon and to stop worrying, adding a heart emoji. *That should keep her happy for a while.*

Flipping the visor down, I open the vanity mirror and groan when I see the bandage over my temple. The cut is small and didn't need stitches, but the doctor said it may leave a scar. Along with the release papers, he gave me instructions on what to look for and the potential side effects of my concussion. Also, a reminder to set up an appointment with my private doctor in two weeks. I was glad he didn't mention the baby while Lance was in the room. I want to be the one to deliver the news about his impending fatherhood, but I'm not sure when or how to do it.

I angle the mirror to look at Rory in the backseat. She is happily singing along with the radio. I catch myself joining her on the chorus of a new country song that's been used recently to advertise a chain restaurant. The song and dance have gone viral and become a social media sensation. Once you hear it, you can't get it out of your head. Even buckled into her car seat, watching her wriggling, and waving her arms above her head to the beat is entertaining.

"Hey little girl, you doing okay back there?" Her eyes light up when she flashes me the familiar smile I never want to lose sight of again.

"Yep," was all she said before going back to singing about *Oreo* shakes with two straws.

As shitty as yesterday was, today has turned out to be pretty amazing. Waking up to see Lance sleeping on the sofa made the butterflies dance wildly in my belly. Or maybe it's our little deputy fluttering already.

"How about you?" I shift in my seat to face him without having to turn my head too much.

"I'm good." This short reply has me taking a closer look. When will he learn I can read him like a book? It's not what he says or even how he says it. It's the blank expression he's worn most of the day that has me concerned. Maybe it's just the severity of everything finally catching up to Lance that has him acting strange. His jaw is tight as he looks from the side mirrors to the rearview then forward again. He's done this several times since we left the hospital and I'm beginning to think there's something he's not telling me.

Look who's talking. I have my own secret that I'm not ready to share either.

The distance from the hospital to my house is relatively short but seems to be taking twice as long as it should. This was great for the first five miles, but now, every bump and pothole Lance rolls over is torture. For what feels like the hundredth time this morning, I have an urgent need to use the bathroom.

"Can you drive any slower?" My change from calm to irritated sarcasm is abrupt, catching Lance off guard.

"Huh? What are you talking about?" Lance slows the truck to stop at a four-way intersection. Even with no cars in sight, he checks and double checks before creeping through at a snail's pace.

"Are you sure you're a cop?" I raise an eyebrow.

"What's that supposed to mean?" He glances in each mirror again then back to me.

"Because cops like to drive fast and you're driving like a little old lady."

"I'm not that slow." He keeps his eyes trained forward and his knuckles turn white as he grips the steering wheel tighter.

"Then what do you call going ten miles below the speed limit and only using the backroads? Are you suddenly afraid of the freeway?"

"I'm just trying to be cautious." He side-eyes me uncomfortably, but I don't want to dive into what's bothering him right now, not when I need him to get a move on. "I mean extra careful, with you and Rory here."

"That's very kind, Mr. Sweet-Talker. But..." I cross my legs and squirm in my seat. "I really need to pee, so can you please hurry up."

"Yes, dear." He chuckles and flashes me a wide grin that makes the sexy little dimple I love pop. He accelerates slightly, but as always seems to happen, the closer we get to my house, the louder nature calls.

"Can't you please go any faster?"

"Is that better?"

Leaning to the side, I look at the speedometer. "Careful there, speed demon. I think you might be going a couple clicks over the limit."

"Oh, now I'm too fast?" He challenges with a cocked brow and lifts his foot off the accelerator.

"No!" I screech. "Keep going."

"Just kidding." He laughs and returns his eyes to the road.

"You're so mean." I roll my eyes and pick up singing along with Rory as a temporary distraction.

Keeping my eyes glued to the prize, I see my house and say a silent prayer when Lance drives as close to my front door as possible.

Mom must have been looking out the window because she rushes out as soon as Lance parks in the driveway. She opens the rear door, unbuckles Rory, and cuddles her close, peppering her with kisses.

"Stay right there." Before I can argue, he is around the front of the truck, helping me climb out of the cab.

"I can open my own door, you know." This heavy-handed, alpha male attitude would be sexy as hell any other time, but I have more important matters to attend to.

"I'm sure you can but humor me." He scoops me up into his arms and strides towards the front door.

"Fine, whatever, but do you think you could walk faster?" His brow furrows and a confused expression settles across his face. "Umm? Remember?"

"Oh, yeah, sorry. I forgot." He practically sprints into the house, then sets me down on my feet in front of the bathroom.

Reaching for the handle, I realize Lance is still staring at me. "Are you going to stand here and wait until I'm done?"

"Uh, no, no. I'll go check on Rory." He shakes his head like he's clearing the cobwebs then turns swiftly towards the living room.

After taking care of business, I tiptoe down the hall to my bedroom to change into something more comfortable than the jeans Lance brought to the hospital. I strip down to just my bra and panties, tossing my clothes into the laundry basket beside the full-length mirror. I catch a glimpse of my reflection and pause to look myself over from head to toe. I place my hands on my hips and look closely at my belly. It's never been muscular or flat. Some may call what I have a slight pooch or the polite version, that I'm curvy. Call it what you want. Either way, I don't think my body will ever look like this again.

After tossing on a pair of old grey sweats and an oversized T-shirt, I slip on some socks and pad down the hall. Mom and Rory are sitting at the small table that is set up for a tea party.

"What took you guys so long to get home?" She looks at her watch. "I expected you a half-hour ago."

"Ask Mr. Putt Putt driver." I hook a thumb towards Lance. "He refused to get on the freeway."

"Do you blame me? I was transporting precious cargo." Lance stands behind me, wraps his arms around my waist, and places soft kisses behind my ear.

"That tickles." I squeal as goosebumps erupt over my entire body.

"I save you, Addy K." Rory giggles and pulls on Lance's arm. "Let go."

We've joked like this before. She loves rushing in to save the day.

"Oh, you want to play too?" Lance lifts her into his arms and kisses her cheek. "Whatcha going to do now?"

She wriggles about as we tickle her belly. "Addy K, stop tickling." Tigress even tries getting in on the action by pawing at my legs.

"Tigress!" Rory shrieks.

Lance places Rory back on her feet so she can play with the cat.

"I missed you sooo much." She picks up Tigress, hugging her tighter than she should. The cat protests with a low growl.

"Be gentle. Tigress doesn't like to be squeezed," I remind

Rory. "Why don't you put her down so we can get ready for lunch?"

"Okay." She loosens her hold and Tigress runs off.

"Rory, can you come with me and help set the table for lunch?" She takes Mom's offered hand, and they stroll into the kitchen.

I sink into the cushions of my oversized chair that sits beside the window and look up to Lance. "Now that it's just us, are we going to talk about what has you so tense?"

"I can't." He lowers his body and kneels beside me, taking my hand in his. "Not yet at least."

"So, it's that bad then?"

He looks out the window then back to me. "I don't know much. I'm waiting for Jackson to call and then I'll tell you what I know."

"You promise you won't keep anything from me?" As much as I want answers, I know I need to trust he will take care of everything and tell me what he can when the time is right.

"I promise." He stands then places the pink fluffy throw blanket over my legs. "Do you need anything before your Dad and I tackle the mounds of gifts in my truck bed?"

"No. I'm good. Mom said lunch will be ready soon."

"Good, I'm starving." Lance lifts the hem of his T-shirt and runs his fingertips over perfectly sculpted abs. Without thinking, I lick my lips. "Erm, my eyes are up here, Babe." Lance's eyes shine with mischief.

"You're trying to distract me, aren't you?" I throw a small pillow at him. "Go. Dad is waiting for you."

His laughter fades as he walks through the front door. The jerk knew exactly what he was doing. I love this playfulness and am happy things seem to be shifting to just another day in our lives.

A flash of fur runs past me, followed by Rory screaming. "Addy K, help me. Tigress is going to kill him."

I look behind the couch and find Tigress is on her back, biting the small stuffed bunny Rory has been toting around lately. It's a battle royal, and Tigress is acting like she's defending her championship belt.

"Bad kitty. Drop it." I reach down to take the toy, but Tigress isn't retracting her sharp claws. Tufts of stuffing are sticking out the bunny's belly. "Tigress, let go." She doesn't listen and continues to bite it. Afraid of pulling too hard and ripping the thin fabric any more than it already is, I tug lightly, but she hangs on tight. A final yank and she lets go, but my actions do what I wanted to avoid and cause more damage. I have the main parts of the body, but before I can grab all the insides, Tigress snatches the puff-ball tail in her mouth like a trophy and races out of the room.

"She broke my bunny." Rory's wail brings Mom from the kitchen.

"Aww, what's happened?" Mom wipes her hands on a kitchen towel and tosses it over her shoulder. "Come here. Let me see."

"Gram Gram, Look." Rory's bottom lip trembles as she hands over the pieces. "Can you fix him?"

"Oh, this isn't so bad. I can have him sewn up lickety-split." Mom lifts Rory's chin. "I'll make him good as new."

"Yay!" Rory jumps up and down. I wish I had an ounce of the energy she has. "Addy K, can I ride my bike?"

"Outside?" A sudden sense of fear and unease I wasn't expecting came over me. Letting her ride her bike around our backyard was never a problem in the past. Now, I feel like I can't take my eyes off her when she plays. "I'm not sure that's a good idea. Maybe tomorrow."

"Why not today?" Rory crosses her arms and stomps her

foot. It's not quite a tantrum, but she's doing a great job of demanding an answer to her question.

"Because…" *I'm afraid someone will take you again.* I try to think of an excuse but come up empty. I want to tell her how scared I am, but she seems unaffected by everything. The last thing I want to do is project my fears onto her when she is dealing with it so well.

As if reading my mind, Mom says, "Kellie, your father and Lance are out there. She'll be fine."

Against my instincts to coddle and protect Rory, I give in, trusting Lance and my dad will watch her. "Fine, but you have to stay in the backyard with Grumpa and Lance." I hold out my arms for a hug and she dives in. I give an extra squeeze and she hurries outside.

"You can't live in fear. I know it hasn't even been a day, but you need to try to go back to living normally, as soon as possible." Mom points to the window. "Look at her." Rory already has her bike helmet held out for my dad to help buckle it.

"How can she be so oblivious to everything that has happened today?"

"Maybe it's because she's surrounded by people who love her. Kids tend to live in the moment. They don't dwell on things the same way we do as adults."

"I guess you're right, but I'm not sure it will be that easy for me to forget or let her out of my sight again."

"Nobody ever said being a parent was easy." She turns her attention back to watching Rory play outside. The oven timer buzzes. "I need to take lunch out of the oven."

"Do you need help?"

"No, dear. You relax." She pats my shoulder and returns to the kitchen.

Finding myself alone again, I intend to take advantage of the quiet moment. I stretch my arms above my head and breathe in deep, then force the air out as I exhale. I close my eyes and focus on deep breathing exercises to calm my nerves.

On my final inhale, I choke as the putrid scent of rotten eggs mixed with sweaty socks hits me. Pinching my nose to keep from inhaling any more of the rancid odor, I walk into the kitchen and instantly regret it.

"Oh, my, God! What is that awful smell?" The acid in my stomach churns and I switch to breathing through my mouth.

"It's your favorite lasagna." Mom cocks her head to the side with a look of concern marring her face.

"Did you burn it or something?" I open the window hoping the breeze will clear the air.

"No, it's just fine. Look?"

She lifts the foil off the tray. It looks great, but the strong smell of garlic and cheese has my stomach twisted in knots. My mouth fills with saliva as bile tries to crawl up my throat. *Could this be morning sickness? I remember Leslie vomiting at all hours of the day for no reason at all.*

"Are you sure you're okay? Maybe I should call the doctor." Mom reaches out and touches my forehead then cheek with the back of her hand. "You don't feel like you have a fever."

"No, I'm fine." I step back from her mothering and the rotten smelling food. "Umm, it's probably just a side effect from the concussion. Maybe I'll go lay down for a bit."

"Oh, okay, go lay down, and I'll bring in a plate of food later. I made that cheesy bread you and your dad like so much." She opens the oven door to remove the bread covered in blue cheese and more garlic and just about lose it right there.

Covering my mouth with both hands, I run towards the bathroom. *Shit, I'm not going to make it.* I barely close the door behind me before emptying the contents in my stomach.

On my knees, I brace myself as I retch violently into the toilet. I hear the door open but am too sick to care who it is. Another wave of nausea kicks in and I swear I'll never cook lasagna again.

"Shh, I'm here." Mom holds my hair back as I continue to retch until nothing is left. She hands me a wet washcloth and puts the lid down for me to sit on. "Better?"

"Yeah. I think so." Reaching into the drawer under the sink, I grab my toothbrush and paste to scrub away the awful taste of vomit. "Wow, I don't know what that was all about."

When I look at my reflection in the mirror, I meet mom's gaze. Her eyes glitter with unshed tears, but she's grinning from ear to ear. "Mom? Why are you smiling?"

I should have known it would be impossible to hide my pregnancy from my mom. Unfortunately, she guesses it right away. The more I tried denying it, the deeper I fell down the rabbit hole until I finally had to give in. I can only hope she will keep my secret until I find the right time to tell Lance.

"I'm so excited." Mom sings and moves around my bedroom while fluffing my pillows.

"Oh, God. Mom, stop, please." Her bouncing around is making me dizzy. "You can't tell anyone, not even Dad."

"Okay, okay, you're right. I'm sorry." She stands perfectly still, clenching her fists and scrunching up her face.

"Is it really going to be that hard for you to keep my secret?" Pulling back the covers on my bed, I lay down and close my eyes until the room quits spinning.

"Yes! I just can't believe my baby is going to have her first baby." She walks around my room fidgeting with different things. She straightens the pictures frames on my bookshelf, then lifts one and stares a little longer than she did the other ones. I know the one she's looking at. It's of Leslie and me at a school carnival. "I can't believe we're going to have another baby," she whispers.

"I was afraid to tell you." It's the first time I admitted this even to myself. "I worried you'd be disappointed that I was irresponsible and got pregnant like Leslie did."

"Babies are always a blessing, even when we don't plan for them." She places the picture back on the shelf and turns to me. "Rory is going to be thrilled to be a big sister."

"Technically, the baby and Rory will be cousins. But maybe it's time to talk about adoption. When we set up a guardianship, it was to ensure I was capable of raising her." I twist my fingers in my lap, still unsure what Mom's reaction will be. There's a small part of me that thinks she and Dad might have doubts after what happened. "In the court's eyes, it was a temporary arrangement. But now, I want to make it official and adopt Rory."

"Your father and I never saw it as temporary. We trusted you from the beginning and still do."

"I know it doesn't really change anything. But when Rory is older, I want her to know I chose to adopt her. I don't want her to think she is any less my child than this little one is." I place my hand over my belly. "Does that make sense?"

"Yes, it makes perfect sense. I think it's a great time to make it official."

"Good, because I want to tell Lance about my plans to adopt Rory at the same time I reveal he's going to be a Daddy. He might as well know what he's getting into if he plans on sticking around."

"I don't think you have anything to worry about. But I'm curious. Why didn't you tell Lance you were pregnant while you were still at the hospital?"

"I don't know. With everything going on, it didn't seem like the right time. Plus, the doctor started talking about all the things that could go wrong with the pregnancy, and I panicked."

"Oh honey, I'm sure everything will be perfect." She brushes back my bangs. "Did they say how far along you are?"

"They did an ultrasound and said they think I'm about seven or eight weeks. Something like that. I was sort of in shock and don't remember much beyond them saying; congratulations, you're going to have a baby." I take a sip of the ginger tea mom made me earlier. She said it helps with nausea and so far, it's working. Mom said she was queasy off and on for the entire nine months with both of her pregnancies. I can only hope I don't have that same experience.

Mom counts on her fingers. "So that means we get to have a Spring baby!"

"Addy K?" Rory's shouting interrupts our moment. She bursts into my room, and within one big leap, she jumps up on the bed. The movement brings back the rolling in my stomach that had finally subsided.

"Don't bounce. Aunt Kellie isn't feeling very good right now." Mom reaches to lift Rory off the bed, but she dodges and snuggles under the covers.

"I want to stay with you." She wraps her arms around my middle and I pull her close.

"I'm going to take a nap. Do you want to lay down with me?" Having her close calms my nerves more than I'd expect.

"Yes."

"Do you need your blanket?"

She nods.

"And Mr. Deputy Bear?"

Another nod.

"Okay, go get them." She scoots off the end of the bed and

out the door, nearly taking out Lance's legs as he enters the room.

"Where's she going?" He looks down the hall.

"To get her blankets and bear."

"Why are you laying down? Are you sick?" He looks between me then my Mom. "Should I call the doctor?" He pulls his phone from his back pocket.

"Oh, she'll be just fine, right?" Mom mouths, *in a few months,* then winks at me.

I glare at her and hope she gets my warning to keep her mouth shut. I get the feeling I'll need to move up my plans to spill the beans before she announces it to everyone who will listen.

"No, no. I'm fine." As if on cue and to prove my point, a genuine sleepy yawn creeps up on me. "I'm just tired."

"Okay, get some rest." He steps up and kisses me gently. "Oh, Jackson asked if he could come by later to get your statement. The Lt. is on at him to finish his report."

"Tell him to come by in a few hours. I want to put this behind us." Another yawn hits and I blink sleepily.

"I'll let him know." Lance steps back and right into Rory's way.

"Excuse me." She scuttles around Lance with her arms full of toys and dragging a blanket behind her.

"Hey, kiddo. Let me help you." Lance lifts her onto the bed and helps get her situated under the covers. He plants a kiss on her forehead. "Take care of Aunt Kellie while I'm gone."

Rory wraps her arms around Lance's neck and squeezes tight. The doctor said she might be a little clingy, so I'm not surprised by her reaction. "Where are you going?"

"I need to go to my house, but I won't be very long." He takes two steps towards the door then turns back. "Oh, I almost forgot. Are you okay having my parents come by for dinner?"

"Yeah, that's fine. It will be nice to see them."

"Great. I'll be back before you wake up. Get some rest."

My eyelids are heavy when he and my mom walk out the door.

"Addy K?" Rory props herself up on her elbow beside me.

"Yes? What's up?" I copy her movements and face her.

She leans in close to my ear and whispers, "I love you," then wraps her arms around my neck.

Her innocent words cut me to the core, and I finally break down. I've been keeping it together in front of everyone, but right now, there's no reason to hold it in.

"I love you more." I sob uncontrollably and allow Rory to comfort me in a way I never imagined my little girl could do. We held each other tight through my silent tears as I whispered, "I love you more, baby. Forever and ever. I love you more."

8

LANCE

"Lance, before you leave, can I talk to you for a moment?" Kellie's mom, Angie, stops me in the hallway and leads me towards the kitchen.

My smile slips away, and I hesitate to answer, immediately concerned my confidence has been breached. When Tom and I spoke at the hospital, we agreed to keep my suspicions about Trish from Angie and Kellie until we are positive she's the one who took Rory. Now I'm wondering if he kept his word or told her after all.

"Sure. What's on your mind?"

"Nothing major." She dishes up a plate of lasagna and hands it to me. "Here, why don't you eat before you go, and we can talk over lunch."

OK, maybe I'm wrong, and letting my constant need to second guess everything get the best of me. It's possible she only wants to feed me the way my mom does when the world is spiraling out of control. In my experience, most mothers tend to think food makes everything better, so it makes sense.

A growling from my stomach reminds me I haven't eaten

today. As much as I want to ignore my hunger, the aroma of spicy tomato sauce and garlic is too inviting to walk away from. I accept the food and take a seat at the table. "This smells delicious, thank you." Taking a bite of the cheese covered pasta, I moan in appreciation.

"I'm glad you like it." She sits across the table from me with her own plate. "It's Kellie's favorite."

"I can see where she gets her extraordinary culinary skills from." I scoop another forkful into my mouth, savoring the homecooked meal.

"That's very kind of you to say." Angie's hands tremble as she unfolds her napkin and lays it across her lap. "I've always enjoyed cooking with my daughters and now passing recipes down to Rory is a joy I never imagined was possible." Her chin dips and shoulders slump as if she's carrying the weight of the world on her shoulders.

Even if by accident, Angie is showing me the vulnerable side of herself I'd guess she keeps hidden from the outside world. From the moment we met, I've admired her strength and the commitment she shows towards her family. Between Leslie's death and watching as her daughter and granddaughter become tied up in recent shocking events would cause even the toughest woman to crumble under this kind of pressure. Yet, she remains the anchor they need to get through the hard times.

Setting my fork down on my plate, I give Angie my full attention. "I don't mean to presume, but it seems like something is on your mind."

"There is, but I don't want to offend or scare you off." Her eyes are still cast downward and her voice wobbles.

"There's no need to hold back." I know better than to jump to conclusions, but as I sit and wait for her to find her words, I wonder if she is going to rake me over the coals since Tom let me off so easy.

"You know Kellie and Rory are my life."

"Yes, of course."

"I've already lost one daughter." She lifts her chin, straightens her back, and sits taller in her chair. "I need you to be honest with me and let me know if they're in any danger." Angie holds my gaze.

Under her scrutiny, my mouth becomes dry, and I find it hard to swallow. Needing a moment, I stall by pouring each of us a glass of lemonade from the pitcher on the table.

"I won't lie to you." I gauge her reaction carefully before continuing. If Tom did share our discussion with her, she gives nothing away. *I said I wouldn't lie, but I don't have to give her all the details.* "I don't have all the information yet, but I would prefer if Kellie and Rory weren't left alone until the investigators finish reviewing security footage from the park and surrounding areas."

Angie places her hand to her chest and gasps. "So, what you're telling me is that you're concerned enough to want them protected, but you can't tell me why."

"Yes. I'm sorry, I wish there was more for me to share, but Jackson isn't telling me everything he knows because I can't be seen to interfere with the investigation."

"So, we just wait?" Angie scowls and tosses her napkin onto her plate.

"Unfortunately, yes. I know asking for your patience doesn't seem fair, but it's the reality of how police investigations work."

She nods a few times as she chews on her bottom lip. As if considering her options carefully, her eyes drift up to the ceiling, then off to the side. I jump as she slaps both hands on the table. "Alright then. We need a plan. I'll set up a schedule. I know my daughter, and if she thinks we are babysitting her, she'll toss us out on our ear."

To say I'm impressed with how she's handling this situation is an understatement. Angie is a true matriarch. I'd hate to see what she might do when Trish is found to be behind Rory's disappearance from the park.

"I agree. Kellie is too independent to let us help, so we need to be creative. I've already spoken to my parents, and they will help as well."

"That's good. It won't look as suspicious if we rotate." She takes her plate and scrapes the food she's barely touched into the garbage. "Finish your lunch. I'll take care of coordinating schedules and you focus on finding the person who's trying to hurt my family."

Pulling into my driveway, I turn off the ignition and finish listening to the ballad I've been playing on repeat. I never paid much attention to lyrics before, but this time the words are too on-point to ignore. It speaks of finding that person that completes you but never imagined existed. Each expression of love during the song makes me think of Kellie and our future. I don't know how many times I've played it, but eventually, I climb out of the truck cab and grab my backpack from the passenger seat.

Opening the front door, I drop the bag on the dining table and lay my jacket over the back of a chair. I'm sure Mom will chew me out if it's still there when she gets home, but I leave it anyway.

My phone buzzes with a text notification. *Speak of the Devil.*

Mom: Dad and I are shopping and plan to meet you at Kellie's for dinner. Please let Angie know we've picked up dessert and a few bottles of wine.

Lance: Okay.

The three dots appear and disappear a few times, indicating she has more to say.

Mom: Is everything alright?

Leave it to my mom to read between the lines of my short answer. She's been a cop's wife for too long. As always, her instincts are dead on. Under normal circumstances, I would have acknowledged her request, but my preoccupation with proving Trish is the only suspect Jackson should be investigating keeps me from being totally present.

Lance: Yeah, I'm fine, just have a lot on my mind. I came home to grab some things, then I'll go back to Kellie's and meet you there.

Mom: You'd tell me if it's become too much for you to handle, right?

There was a time I'd be angry about her assuming I'm not able to deal with any extra stress. But she knows how low I was after Paul's death. Her emotional check in makes me think hard about where my headspace is right now, and even though this feels like a waking nightmare, I can confidently say I'm nowhere near that same depressed state of mind now. In fact, I'm in fight or flight mode, which is probably what is keeping those feelings at bay. It's a good reminder to look up the dates for a peer support meeting and attend one soon.

Lance: I promise. Right now, I'm doing alright. Thanks for checking.

Mom: That's what Moms do.

Not all moms are as in tune with their children. If we were face to face, I have no doubt she would have me wrapped up tight in her arms and fighting off tears. I'm incredibly fortunate to have such amazing parents and don't know what I'd do without them. My phone vibrates again, and I look to see another text from my mom.

Mom: Sorry. Dad wants to remind you he's here to help if he can.

I'm sure just like me, Dad's itching to get deeper into the evidence. They aren't going to let him in on the case any more than they will me, but maybe he and I can talk about what I know and see what we come up with. After all, Dad was one of the best investigators in his department. *Once a cop, always a cop.*

Lance: Tell him thanks.

Mom: Great. See you soon. We love you, son.

She adds three heart emoji's—black, blue, and another black, symbolizing the thin blue line.

Lance: Love you, too.

Her text takes some of the weight I've been carrying off my shoulders. My plan to have our parents guard Kellie and Rory removes a sliver of worry, but not all of it. My instincts tell me Trish is lying in wait for the perfect moment to strike again, so having family nearby is the best deterrent I can think of for now.

I rub the back of my neck and shoulders, feeling the tightness in each muscle. Thinking about that bitch has my temples throbbing with the onset of a headache. Pulling my shirt over my head, I decide a long shower might help, hoping the hot water will relax the muscles. Stripping down completely, I lazily leave my clothes in a pile at the foot of my bed.

Turning the shower setting to full, I allow the water to warm. Before I can step under the spray, the muffled sound of my phone ringing comes from my pants still lying on the floor. I hurry to shut off the water and dig through my clothes until I find it. "Hey, Jackson. Do you have any updates for me?"

"Nothing new." His monotone response leads me to believe he's got more and not telling me. "How are you doing?"

"As good as can be expected, I guess. I'm at home right now. I grab a pair of loose basketball shorts and pull them on, then amble towards my kitchen for something to relieve my headache.

"And what about Kellie and Rory. Are her parents still with them?"

I search through the cabinet, find the pills, and grab a water glass. "Yeah. Angie and I spoke a little bit about my plan. She's setting up a schedule, so they won't be left alone."

"That's good because we still don't have anything concrete to go on."

"Has Trish even been questioned yet?" I pop the pills into my mouth and take a long drink of water to wash them down.

"Not yet. The Sheriff specifically instructed me to wait until we have more evidence than just your accusation."

"So, he doesn't believe me." I shake my head, frustrated that I'm not able to help in any way.

"That's not true. You know we all have your back, and I won't let anyone, including you, fuck it up."

"Yeah, whatever." I slam the cabinet door and stomp back to my bedroom.

"Knock off the asshole attitude and realize we're on the same team." He cautions. "I'll be at Kellie's around six. Do you plan to be there?"

"Like I'd let you question them without me being there." My eyes are drawn to an envelope propped up on the pillows lying on my bed. I don't remember seeing it there when I walked in earlier. There's no stamp, just Lance written in block letters across the front.

"I'm warning you for the last time. Keep your distance and let me do my job."

"Fine, just keep it low key, and if Rory gets agitated, I'm cutting you off. She's been through enough and seems to have already forgotten the whole thing."

"Give me some credit. I've got more years on you and know how to do my job."

I switch over to the speakerphone and set it beside me so I can open the envelope. Inside is a picture of Rory from yesterday at the park. It's from before she was taken while she laughed and played with her friends.

Jackson continues to ramble on about something, but I pay no attention to what he's saying.

Turning the picture over, I see the message written in a black permanent marker.

She's such a sweet little girl. It would be terrible to lose her again.

"Fuck, Jackson!" I bellow, ready to explode. "You need to get over here right now."

"What's wrong?"

"She was just in my house." A growl rumbles up from my chest and I look around the room thinking maybe she'd be stupid enough to still be here.

"Slow down. Who are you talking about?"

"Who do you think? Trish." I grab the phone and storm through my house, looking through closets and opening every door to a place she might be hiding. "I found an envelope in my room. It has a picture of Rory and a message. She's playing games and it ends right now." Balling up my hand, I put my fist through the wall.

"Wait for us to get there. I'm only about fifteen minutes away from your house." I recognize the sound of his cruiser engine revving and then shifting hard while he speeds to get here.

"Fine, but if you're any longer, I'm outta here and handling it myself." I disconnect the call just as his siren pierces through down the line.

My hand throbs from punching the wall and I notice blood dripping from cuts on my knuckles. I stomp into the kitchen for ice and a towel to wrap around my hand and freeze when I see all the artwork Rory made for me scattered on the floor.

"What the fuck?" Minutes ago, they were hung perfectly on the refrigerator. I leave them there as evidence but notice one picture has been ripped in half. It's the one of me, Kellie, and Rory holding hands in front of their house with huge smiles on our faces. I'm sure it's no accident that it has been torn in such a way that it separates them from me. Trish may think she's smart, but I will find a way to finish the game she started.

Jackson and Sergeant Williams took over an hour to finish

searching for and gathering evidence from inside my house. Unfortunately, aside from the letter and torn pictures, there wasn't any indication someone had even been in the house.

After double checking with my parents about locking up before they left, Mom admitted she might have left a window open in their room. Jackson dusted for prints and lifted a few, but my guess Trish's won't be identified.

My anger simmers at the surface while I drive back to Kellie's but fades the minute I walk through the door.

"Lance." Rory runs towards me and crashes into my legs. I lift her up high and swing her in a circle before placing her back on the ground. "Come color with me." She takes my hand and leads me over to her table. A stack of blank paper and a box of broken crayons sit in the middle.

"Whoa, hang on a minute. I need to talk with Auntie Kellie first."

"Pweeze, Lance?" She lowers her chin and looks up at me with puppy dog eyes then pokes out her bottom lip. This little girl has me whipped.

Just as I'm about to cave, Kellie walks into the room and stops me. "Don't do it." She smirks and leans against the wall with her arms crossed over her chest. "Be strong."

"Uh, umm, now Rory, you need to be patient." I glance at Kellie for support as she nods her approval. "I'll play with you once I talk to your Aunt."

"Okay." Rory sulks over to her table and begins drawing quietly by herself.

"Good job, Deputy. I'm proud of you." Kellie strolls casually up to me and wraps her arms around my neck. "You're getting better. Last week you would have given in without hesitating."

"That was harder to do than getting a drunk inside a cab at 2am on a Saturday night."

"Why does that not surprise me." Kellie tosses her head back and laughs. "You're putty in her hands."

"Yeah, I am." I look over my shoulder and see Rory is too engrossed in her coloring to pay us any attention. I gently kiss the bandage on her forehead, then the tip of her nose, and finally her soft lips. "I'm putty in your hands, too."

Kellie kisses me passionately. I pull her body snug against mine, taking full advantage of having her in my arms.

"Erm," a male voice interrupts. We turn our heads to find my dad hovering.

"Can I help you, Dad?" I ask, not caring that he just witnessed me enjoying what I thought was a private moment with my girlfriend.

"Uh, your mothers' asked me to find out what kind of salad dressing you want." The corners of his mouth turn up.

"Really? Or did they send you in to spy?" I arch a brow and stare him down. My father has always been a straight shooter so telling this little lie is an impossible task.

"I'll just tell them ranch dressing. As you were." He turns on his heel and sings something about young love while leaving the room.

"Having both sets of parents here might be a problem." Kellie steps out of my arms and leads me over to Rory.

"Or it could work out perfectly for us." I wiggle my eyebrows. "Built in babysitters."

Jackson and I decided it was best not to discuss the incident at my house until after he questions Trish. He and Javier have an appointment with the head of the rehab facility in the morning, then plan on meeting with Trish immediately after.

I was glad when Jackson announced he was finished recording Kellie's statement. Thankfully it didn't take too long because even though Rory had a nap, she was ready for bed earlier than usual but wanted Kellie to read her a story first.

"Good night, everyone." Jackson gathers his things and zips up his bag.

"Are you sure you can't stay for dessert?" Angie asks.

"How about some wine?" My mom adds with a lopsided smile. I've never seen her this tipsy before. It was good to see her and Angie chatting like old friends over dinner, but they may have overindulged a bit.

"Uh, no, thank you. Maybe another time." Jackson looks at me and smirks.

"I'll take more wine." Angie raises her full glass.

"Mom, your glass is already filled to the brim." Kellie shakes her head. "I think you've probably had enough."

"No way. Tracy and I are celebrating." Angie winks.

"You two have been acting strange all night." My eyes dart between the two as they feign innocence. "What gives?"

"That's for us to know and you to find out." My mom burst out laughing at her childish joke. "Right, Gram Gram?" She clinks her glass against Angie's and they both giggle like young schoolgirls.

"Don't mind them. They're hammered and have no idea what they're saying." Kellie's cheeks are pink, making me wonder if she's had a few glasses of wine with our mom's. Or maybe tonight has taken a toll on her. She didn't eat much and excused herself from the table a few times to use the restroom.

"Are you okay? You look flushed." I touch her cheek and feel the heat on my palm.

"I'm fine." She pulls away quickly. "Thank you, Jackson, for coming here instead of having us come to the station. It made it a lot easier, especially for Rory."

"You're very welcome. I'll be in touch." Jackson turns to leave, and I follow.

"Hey, Dad. Can you take care of them while I walk Jackson outside?" I point to the mom's, and he rolls his eyes.

"Come on, ladies. How about some coffee with our dessert?" Dad and Tom each guide their wives into the kitchen.

"We can't celebrate with coffee. Besides, it says on the bottle; it's a dessert wine." Mom laughs again and links arms with Angie. Those two are definitely up to something.

Jackson pops the trunk and puts his laptop bag inside. "If you're expecting me to share what Kellie told me, you're wasting your time."

"I wasn't going to ask, but if you're offering…" He shakes his head. "It was worth trying."

"Go back inside with your family and try to forget about the case for tonight." He closes the trunk and circles around to the driver's side door.

"Yeah, sure. I may have a smile on my face, but inside I'm still on the job." My mind won't shut down until Trish is arrested and then prosecuted. "This isn't easy, Jackson. But they are my life now and I need to protect them."

"I know," he agrees, "and it's why you have a plan in place to keep someone with them at all times."

"I think I'm going to talk to my dad and Tom tonight. Get them on the same page since Tom already knows my suspicions."

"That's not a bad idea. Your dad, especially since he will probably be the biggest help, but I suggest you keep it from Kellie and both moms until it's absolutely necessary to tell them."

"I agree. I think Angie would march right over to the rehab facility and rip Trish out of there so fast her head would spin."

"Yeah, and your mom would be right beside her. I get the feeling they could cause some serious damage when protecting their family."

"Just be glad they're on our side."

"I am." He chuckles. "I need to get out of here. You're working tomorrow, right?"

"Yeah. Back on day shift, for the next month. That is if they don't change it to cover when someone is out. I wish we could hire more deputies and quit being so shorthanded."

"You and me both." He opens his car door and waves over his shoulder, then drives away.

When I come back inside the house, everyone is in the living room, watching a movie and eating dessert.

"Here, Lance. Come sit beside Kellie." Mom scoots over on the couch to sit closer to Dad.

Kellie smiles sheepishly and offers me her cake. "Here you go."

"You're not going to eat it?"

"No, my stomach still isn't right. Probably from the medicine they gave me at the hospital." She picks up the fork, breaks off a corner of the cake, and feeds it to me. "It's all yours."

"I never turn down cake." I accept the plate and dig in. "What are we watching?"

"Your mom picked the movie." Dad rolls his eyes. "Some romantic comedy called Knocked Up."

"It's one of my favorites!" Angie shouts a little too loud.

"Mine too," Mom says and they both start giggling again.

"Shh, did you forget your granddaughter is asleep?" It's Kellie's turn to play the responsible parent.

"Sorry," they stage whisper in unison, then cackle uncontrollably.

Remembering to keep my voice low, I lean in close to

Kellie so only she can hear. "Our moms should not be allowed to play together."

"Yeah, but I don't think that's an option." Kellie snickers.

"I think you're right." I wrap one arm around Kellie and focus on how lucky I am. Tomorrow will be different, but right now, life seems perfect.

9

KELLIE

"Just five more minutes, please," I beg as the intro to Cyndi Lauper's *Girls Just Want To Have Fun* plays from my phone, waking me from a restless sleep. With my eyelids half-open, I fumble around, then lean over and peer under my bed where the music is coming from. Practically falling headfirst onto the floor, my fingertips brush the phone case. Hanging precariously off the edge of the mattress with my legs twisted up in the sheets, I stretch until I'm finally able to pick it up. Pressing snooze, I drop my phone onto the now vacant side of the bed.

I stare up at the ceiling and try to let go of the tension surrounding the decision following last night's conversation. After a heated discussion with my family, I made the hard decision to stand strong and refuse to play the victim. I've placed my full trust in the Springhill Sheriff's Department to find whoever it was that took Rory and vow to not allow this mystery person to dictate how we live our lives. This included the decision for Rory to return to preschool.

Our parents were hesitant but eventually agreed with me. On the other hand, Lance insisted it was a bad idea but waited until we were in bed to voice all of his concerns. Although he's not Rory's father, I listened intently to everything he said. I'd prefer we were on the same page, but ultimately the choice is mine to make.

"This wasn't an easy decision, Lance. I'm going to be a nervous wreck, but Rory needs to be a normal kid, and that means going to school."

"I know, but can't you keep her home until we know who took Rory?" He sits down on his side of the bed and removes his boots. Each one hits the hardwood floors with a heavy thud.

"No, Lance, we can't, and locking her up inside this house to keep her safe isn't healthy. You need to think about this from my point of view." His concerns are legitimate, but that doesn't stop me from arguing for what I feel is right.

"I'm not trying to lock either of you up." He stands, then runs his hand over the back of his neck. "Do you have any idea how hard it's going to be while I'm at work, knowing I can't protect you if this person shows up again?"

"I'm sure, but it's gonna be just as hard for me when you go to work and I'm alone." I allow my words to sink in then go to the bathroom to take off my makeup and change into my pajamas.

When I return to my room, he's standing by the window with his arms crossed over his chest. "Can you at least wait until she—" His mouth snaps shut. I watch Lance closely as he takes a minute to school his expression. When he looks at me once more, his face gives nothing away of his true feelings. "What I mean is, can you please wait until the person who took Rory is found?"

"And what if they never find that person. What would you have us do then? I don't want to feel afraid for the rest of my life." My tone is soft because I'm not angry with him. I know Lance loves Rory and only wants to ensure she's safe.

Even in the moonlight, I can see him mulling over my words carefully. The protective side of him doesn't want to concede, but he can't deny there is some truth to what I've said.

I slide under the covers and wait in the silence.

After several minutes, he strips down to just his boxer briefs and lays down on the bed beside me. "At least let me go to the school and ask about their security protocols before she returns."

Finally, he's given me something I can work with. "If that will put your mind at ease, then I think it's a great plan."

I lay my head on his chest and listened as the rhythm of his heartbeat soothed me. Neither of us got exactly what we wanted and that's okay because every relationship requires give and take.

I'm not sure either of us got much sleep. Lance tossed and turned all night while I stared up at the ceiling, willing my brain to shut off. Each time I closed my eyes, two things would jerk me awake. First, how, and when do I tell Lance I'm pregnant and am I making the right decision about sending Rory to school?

At some point, I gave up on trying to find answers to those difficult questions and allowed some good memories to filter in and out of my dreams. From Leslie with her round belly, ready to give birth to Rory, to watching that silly movie with my family last night. Thinking about happier times allowed me to doze off briefly until Lance's phone vibrated on the nightstand at 3am.

Before he left for work, he kissed my cheek and whispered, "I love you." I pretended to be asleep, knowing if I'd replied, I would have pleaded with him to stay, and I have no doubt he would have tried calling into the station wanting another day off.

Asking Lance to choose between his job or staying home with me is selfish, but I have a feeling this will be something I'll struggle with daily. An unending cycle of worrying when he walks out the door and sigh of relief when he returns home safe. While he's working, I can't seem to stop the negative from seeping into my mind. It's been the same fear since we started dating. Only this morning, my worries included how our baby's life would be affected should something terrible happen while he's on patrol. *What if today is the day he doesn't come home and now I'm left to raise two children alone?*

Just as my eyelids start to feel heavy, the same annoying song plays, and I scramble to press snooze once more.

I don't think I've ever felt this exhausted in my life.

Rolling onto my back, I rub my eyes then open my phone to check the time. It's barely 6am.

If Rory stays on her routine, she'll be awake in an hour wanting breakfast. I'm not sure I have the energy to climb out of bed, let alone make the pancakes and sausage she's been eating each morning for the past few weeks. Her appetite has increased again, making me think she's going through yet another growth spurt, which means another shopping trip for bigger clothes.

Opening the app on my phone that I use to manage what I need to do each day, I scroll through the ever-growing list and add shopping for Rory to the bottom. Most of today's tasks are simple everyday chores like laundry, vacuuming, and general tidying up the house. If I'm too tired, I can always push those back a day or two. There's no delaying the next one on the list, though.

"Gross," I complain when I see the reminder to clean the litter box. I love Tigress, but this job is the one I dread the most. With my recently heightened sense of smell, the mere thought of catching a whiff of cat pee is all it takes to make me gag.

But wait, there may be a way out of this grotesque assignment. I remember reading an article a few years ago while waiting for an annual appointment to see my OB/GYN. It said something about how changing litter can be dangerous during pregnancy. I'll need to look that tidbit up, and if it's true, I will happily hand this awful chore over to Lance.

I scroll to the top of the list and see the two priority items that had me tossing and turning most of the night.

The first one is my call the preschool. I need to arrange a meeting about their security systems and protocols and confirm they are ready for her to return. Other than coordinating with Lance so he can attend, it seems simple enough. It will also allow me to update Rory's files to add Lance's parents as approved adults for drop-off and pick-up.

The next task will be how to tell Lance he's going to be a Daddy. Now that Mom figured out I'm pregnant, I can't delay any longer because she's the worst at keeping secrets. I suspect Mom already spilled the beans to Tracy. It's only a matter of time before they let it slip to someone else. I can't let Lance find out from anyone other than me.

I've stalled getting out of bed long enough. "Get your lazy butt up," I chastise myself. Throwing the covers off my body, I sit up too quickly and feel dizzy. It was a huge mistake. I blink several times, trying to focus, but the room spins.

My stomach lurches. "Oh, no, not again." Dashing into the bathroom, I wrap my arms around my belly as wave after wave of dry heaves racks my body.

I was too nauseous to eat more than a few bites at dinner. The pungent odor wafting through the air from what is usually my favorite food was an assault on my senses, forcing me to rush to the bathroom twice. Thankfully, everyone put it down to the aftereffects of suffering a concussion. I was happy to let them believe it.

"Honey, are you okay?" Mom peeks her head inside my bathroom door.

"I think I'm going to die." I retch again as tears flow down my cheeks.

With my head still hung over the toilet bowl, I hear the soft click of the door closing. Mom sweeps my hair back from my face. "I suppose it's time to share the little tricks every new mommy-to-be needs to know."

"Bring it on." I sit on the tile floor of the bathroom and lean against the tub for support. "Will they keep me from praying to the porcelain goddess every few hours because I don't think I can do this every day?"

"Not completely, but it should help," she replies.

"Go on."

"For starters, jumping out of bed on an empty stomach is a big no-no. You need to keep ginger ale and crackers nearby. It's not foolproof, but it helps. And as you've already figured out, sickness can come any time of the day."

"No kidding, what else?" I grab a handful of tissues from the box cabinet beside the sink and blow my nose

"Oh, there's a lot of them. You won't need to worry about it just yet, but before you reach your third trimester, I suggest a map with all the best restrooms while you're away from home."

"Why would I need a map?"

"Because the baby will be sitting on your bladder and when you gotta go, you gotta go." She cringes. "I learned the hard way."

"Did you pee yourself?"

"Many times."

"Great, so you're telling me I get to look forward to more barfing and that I'll eventually pee myself," I whine, acting more like a little girl with her Mommy taking care of her than a grown woman having a baby. "Pregnancy sounds like an absolute blast." I hang my head feeling defeated. *This is not at all what I was expecting.*

She places her fingers under my chin, lifting my head up so I can look into her eyes. "Just wait. The first time you hear your baby's heartbeat and feel the light flutters in your belly, you'll forget everything else." Mom holds out her hand and I accept her help getting up off the floor. "But I'm not going to lie to you because labor and giving birth hurts like hell."

"Gee, thanks, Mom."

"And don't believe the hype about forgetting the pain after you give birth. I never did, but I promise it was still worth it. After all, I did it twice." Mom wipes away a stray tear that slipped down her cheek. Undoubtedly another memory of Leslie has wormed its way into her thoughts just as it did mine. It tugs hard on my heartstrings when I think about not having my sister with me during my pregnancy.

"I guess I'll just have to follow your lead." I stand in front of the vanity mirror and stare at my reflection. My pale skin only accentuates the dark circles under my eyes. "You're the expert."

"Trust me, I'm no expert and made plenty of mistakes. I had to learn most things the hard way." She kisses my cheek. "But remember, you're not alone. Tracy and I are here for you to lean on."

"I know." I hug her tight then pull away, remembering something important. "Hey, I almost forgot to ask. Did you tell Tracy that I'm pregnant?" I wait for her answer.

"Nope," she says while avoiding my gaze.

"Then what was all that Gram Gram talk about and your choice of the movie last night? Knocked Up? Real subtle, Mom." I swish my mouth out with water, look into the mirror, and see her behind me, straightening the stack of towels.

"I didn't tell her." She turns to me with a sheepish grin. "But Tracy guessed, and I didn't bother telling her she was wrong."

"Mom," I huff out. "You promised you'd wait until I spoke to Lance."

"I did, technically. Besides, Tracy promised she would keep our secret."

"Just like you did, huh?"

"Well, hurry up and tell Lance so we can all celebrate."

I count to ten so I don't snap at her. "Fine. I already planned to tell him tonight." An idea springs to mind, but it will take some help from Gina and Melanie. "Do you think you can take Rory out for dinner so I can do something special for Lance?"

"Yes! Just leave everything to me. I'll invite David and Tracy to join us too."

"Wait, maybe I should rethink this." I squeeze the bridge of my nose when I imagine the trouble Tracy and my mom could get into.

"No, you have to do it tonight," Mom blurts out.

"Fine, but do I need to remind you to wait for Lance to know before Dad and David are told?"

She puckers her lips and pretends to turn a key and toss it over her shoulder.

"Not good enough." I shake my head. "I want to hear the words."

"Fine." She rolls her eyes. "I promise I won't tell the Grandpa's about the new baby."

"And I'm holding you responsible for making sure Lance's mom keeps her mouth closed as well."

"Got it." She salutes me and I see the corners of her mouth turn up.

"Good. Now I have a lot to do. While I take a shower, can you please get Rory's breakfast?" A gurgle erupts from my stomach when I mention food, and for a second, I think I might vomit again.

"Of course." She closes the door behind her.

Stripping out of my pajamas, I climb into the shower and think about the new things I need to add to my list to pull off my plan.

"Ready or not, Sir Lancelot. You're about to get one hell of a surprise."

Knowing Mom and Dad would take care of Rory until I emerged from my room, I didn't rush, staying under the spray until the water ran cold. After a quick blowout of my hair to make it manageable, I pull it back into a ponytail and apply a touch of makeup. A final inspection in the full-length mirror and I conclude I look less like a zombie than I did earlier and am ready to face the day.

Stepping into the kitchen, Rory and both sets of grandparents are eating their breakfast. I don't think they see me, so I back pedal and peek around the corner from the hallway to spy.

"Where would you like to have dinner tonight?" Mom directs her question to Rory, who is busy shoveling fruit-flavored loop cereal into her mouth.

"I don't know." She mumbles while chewing.

"Don't talk with your mouthful." Mom gently scolds.

Rory swallows then taps her finger against her chin. I do it subconsciously when thinking and it's something she still likes to imitate. "Helen's."

"Fantastic choice," Dad says, beaming at his grand-daughter.

"Sounds perfect to me." David nods his approval.

"What do you think, Kellie?" Tracy looks right at me and offers a warm smile.

"That I've been busted." I turn the corner and join them at the table, sitting in the empty chair next to Rory. "Good morning."

"Morning, Addy K." Rory reaches out, and I take her into my arms, allowing her to sit on my lap. I inhale slowly and am grateful when the aroma from the bacon, eggs, and fried potatoes doesn't turn me green around the gills.

"So, are you enjoying having breakfast with your grandparents?" I reach for a slice of toast from a plate in the middle of the table. Testing my appetite, I nibble a corner and swallow, expecting it to climb back up my throat like everything else has lately. When my stomach doesn't immediately reject the food, I take a bigger bite and pour myself some juice.

"Yes, and Gram Gram said we could go to Helen's and then I can sleep over."

"No, I said we will ask Aunt Kellie if you can spend the night with us after we have dinner." Mom corrects her. I rarely say no to Rory staying with my parents, but I appreciate my mom not assuming and waiting for my approval.

"You know what?" I take a sip to wash down the dry toast. "I think that's a great plan. I have something important I need to do tonight and not having to rush will make it a lot easier."

"Yay!" Rory climbs down from my lap. "I'll go pack."

"I'll help." Mom trails right behind her.

"They might need an extra hand." Tracy stands and follows Mom out of the kitchen.

"And off they go." Dad's belly shakes with laughter. "They've been acting bizarre all morning."

"You know," David looks to my dad. "If I didn't know any better, I'd say our wives are up to something."

"You wouldn't by chance have any idea why they are acting so strange, would you, Kellie?" Dad tilts his head, and I nearly spit the juice I was drinking across the table.

He has always been a human lie detector when it comes to me, so instead of answering, I shrug then shove another piece of toast in my mouth. Dad continues to stare in my direction while I chew until there's nothing left.

Tom turns his chair to face me. "Kellie, you know my job for over twenty years was to seek the truth and interrogate suspects, right?"

Shit. I've never been a good liar and now I'm under the eagle eye of a trained detective.

Sweat covers my upper lip and I chew on my thumbnail while searching for an escape route. "Uh oh. I think I hear Rory calling me?" I turn my head and pretend to listen. "I'm coming. Sorry, but Rory needs me." As if a fire was lit under my butt, I race out of the kitchen to the backyard. I'll be glad when everyone knows I've got a bun in the oven, and I don't have to hide anymore.

Instead of going back inside to help Rory pack, I wander around the yard. It's a beautiful day full of white puffy clouds that stand out against the vibrant blue sky. Out of nowhere, a memory pops into my head from when Leslie and I were young. It seems to happen a lot lately.

She and I used to love laying on our backs and letting our imaginations run wild, looking up at the different shapes, then calling out what each one looked like. We never agreed, each of us seeing something different. Tilting my head back, I spot an odd, shaped cloud and watch as it slowly morphs into the image of a dragon spitting fire. I can almost hear Leslie correcting me, probably saying it looks more like an elephant blasting water into the sky. I can only hope Rory and this baby will be as close as Leslie and I were. Strolling over the dew-covered grass towards the bench my dad placed in the garden, I pull my phone from my pocket and sit down to search for fun ways to announce a pregnancy to the father. Scrolling through some images, my eyes fixate on one that I think will be perfect.

∾

Dad insisted it was common knowledge that a person hospitalized due to a concussion shouldn't drive for at least forty-eight hours. Rather than argue with him, I called Melanie and Gina for a ride to the mall.

I'd initially planned to have them meet me there to get some input on how to tell Lance. But when I finally started thinking clearly, I decided too many people already knew before him, and it's best I figure it out on my own.

Either way, it was good to get out with friends, especially after the conversation Lance and I had about staying home. I was talking about Rory, but I caught his comment about keeping us both safe. It wasn't a slip of the tongue. He is constantly worried about both of us.

While Gina and Melanie shopped for dresses they needed for an upcoming family party, I pretended to need to use the bathroom and snuck over to the baby section to make my purchase. Then, I hurried over to another store to have it personalized. When I returned to the women's department, they'd just finished paying for their items and were none the wiser.

When I returned home, Mom and Tracy shooed me away from the kitchen, insisting I take a nap, so I did just that. Waking a few hours later, I check my phone and notice I've missed a text.

Lance: On my way.

He sent it at 6pm and it's 6:21 pm now. I sit up slowly, just like mom said to do, and am pleasantly surprised that the trick worked. The sleeve of crackers and can of ginger ale are close by, just in case. When I swing my legs over the side of the bed, I realize I'm starving but want something more than just crackers because I haven't consumed much in the past few days.

When Melanie insisted we take a break for lunch at the mall, I gave in and ordered a beef gyro from the Greek take-out place. The first few bites were delicious, but I decided I shouldn't push my luck and tossed half of it in the garbage. Now my stomach is growling to be fed, so I search for a light snack before dinner.

"Hey, Mom. What time are you leaving to take Rory to dinner?" I open the pantry door and take a handful of dry cereal straight from the box.

"That depends. When's Lance due to be home?"

"It looks like he got off on time for a change." I look at the time on my phone once more. "I expect him any minute."

"We aren't in any rush, dear." Tracy wipes the kitchen counter with a dishtowel. She and Mom insisted on helping set up dinner while I focused on getting myself ready. "You should relax. I'll let you know when Lance gets here."

"I've already taken a nap. You guys take off and I'll finish up in here."

Dad enters the kitchen and kisses mom on the cheek. "Sorry, Kellie, but we can't leave yet. The game is in extra innings."

"We have a bet on which team is going to choke first." David comes in and grabs a bottle of water from the refrigerator.

"Oooh, you're right. That is more important than my dinner with Lance." My voice drips with sarcasm, earning a stern look from my dad. I'm not usually this sassy, but the anticipation and anxiety of how Lance will handle my big announcement are taking their toll on me.

"What does the winner get?" Mom asks, successfully defusing the situation.

"It's what the loser gets that's important. Rory can tell you." David calls her and she dashes in wearing her favorite pink tutu and tiara. "Tell Addy K what the prize is."

"The winner gets to dress up and do ballet with me." Raising her hands into the air above her head like a prima ballerina, she tiptoes in a circle. She's been asking to take ballet class ever since Tracy bought her this playset.

"And what else?" David encourages.

"I get to put makeup on the winner and have a princess tea party." She jumps up and down excitedly, clapping her hands.

"That sounds like a great prize." Lance's deep voice startles me.

"How long have you been standing there?" When I turn around, my tongue practically rolls out of my mouth. Seeing him in uniform will never fail to make me weak at the knees. He's hotter than any superhero I've ever watched on the big screen.

Lance bends to lift Rory into his arms. "Hi, beautiful girl. Did you have a good day?"

Rory nods, looking at Lance like he holds the moon and stars.

I wonder if that's how I look when I stare into his eyes.

Tracy slides up beside me and whispers, "I get it. There's nothing like the sight of your officer walking through the door after a shift." I follow her gaze until it lands on her husband. "Part of me still misses those days." She hip checks me and casually strolls up beside David, linking her arm around his.

"I've got a better idea. Why don't both grandfathers plan a dress-up party with Rory?" Tracy suggests and all the color drains from their faces.

"I agree. They'll look great in matching tutus." Mom smirks then hides behind the dishcloth she's holding.

"What about you, Lance? Should we buy you a tutu as well?" Tracy challenges.

Without missing a beat, Lance says. "I'm in." Then he

blows a raspberry on Rory's cheek before handing her off to me.

"Well, now that Lance is here, I guess we should be going." David hot foots it into the living room, calling over his shoulder. "Tom, bring Rory with you before Tracy comes up with any wilder ideas."

"Got it." Dad takes Rory's hand. "Come with Grumpa and we can finish getting ready for dinner and your sleepover."

Laughter fills the kitchen as they hurry to escape. I'll bet Tracy has new tutus ready by Monday for their impending tea party.

"I guess the game wasn't so important after all," I mumble to myself.

"Now it's your turn to get ready for dinner." Tracy points at Lance. "Kellie's been cooking up a storm for you, so get ready, and we'll get out of your hair."

"Sounds good to me." He takes a few steps towards the hall before turning to look back at me. "I'm going to take a shower first. Wanna join me?" He sports a wicked smile and playfully wiggles his eyebrows.

"You did not just say that in front of our mothers." Totally caught off guard and flustered, I drop my voice. Heat rises and my cheeks flame. I shoot a look at our moms, who are staring back with amusement glittering in their eyes.

"I'll take a rain check." He winks, then walks away with an arrogant yet playful swagger I've never seen before. I continue to stare in the direction he sauntered off in, feet glued to the floor and utterly speechless.

"He's just as flirtatious and embarrassing as his father." Tracy pats my arm. "But don't worry, you'll get used to it."

"Bye, Rory. Be good for Gram Gram and Grumpa," I call out

from the porch while my dad pulls out of the driveway. While Lance was in the shower, I wrapped his gift and stashed it under the dining table so I could give it to him at the ideal moment.

"So, it's just us tonight," Lance says from behind me. I sense the disappointment in his tone. He loves having dinner and watching movies with Rory, but I've learned it's important to have time to ourselves as well. Fortunately, we have the luxury many don't. Having both sets of parents ready and willing to help is more than we could ever ask for.

"Yep, just us." Closing the front door, I turn towards the sound of his voice. *Holy shit!* The sight of him earlier in his uniform almost knocked me on my ass. Seeing him in a black T-shirt that stretches over his muscular chest and low slung, grey sweatpants showing off that perfect v from hip to hip might kill me.

"I can work with that." He slides his arms around my waist and nuzzles my neck. The scent of his skin is fresh and slightly woodsy from the body wash I bought him.

I tilt my head to the side, giving him better access to the place I love to have kissed, right behind my ear.

"We have to stop. I have a special dinner planned for us."

"Don't you think dinner can wait?"

"No, it can't." I slide out from his embrace and walk to the kitchen on unsteady legs. "Go sit down and I'll set the table." Of course, Lance doesn't listen and follows me so he can help. "Fine, you can carry the big tray, and I'll be right behind you with the rest."

"This is a lot of food. Did you cook all day?" He places the tray in the middle of the table.

"Truth? Our moms wouldn't let me do anything." Lance tips his head back and laughs heartily. "They did all the cooking, so I have no idea what's under these covers."

"Our moms are terrific cooks. I'm sure it will be great."

He pulls out my chair. I try to sit gracefully, but my nerves kick in, and I almost knock over the box near my feet. Lance must have noticed me tense up. "Not that something you cooked wouldn't have tasted great."

"Oh, I'm not bothered by that. They could give a Michelin star chef a run for their money."

Lance removes the cover from the tray and inhales. "Yum, I knew I recognized that smell. My mom's famous baby back ribs." He places three on my plate and then his own. "Is that enough?"

"Yeah, thanks." The smell isn't as pleasant for me.

"What else do we have?" Lance opens two covered bowls and fills his plate.

When I see what the side dishes are, I almost choke.

Baby potatoes, carrots, and squash. Another bowl has a salad with a variety of baby greens. Oh, and heaven forbid they miss the baby-sized corn muffins.

Utterly oblivious to the subliminal messages staring him in the face, Lance continues to load up his plate with the tiny vegetables.

"I didn't have time for more than a candy bar today. I'm starving." He lifts a rib to his mouth and seems to savor each bite while I poke at the food with a fork, wondering if I'll be able to consume any of it.

"Aren't you hungry?" Lance gestures to my untouched plate of food.

"Uh, yeah, I'm starving. I'm just trying to figure out where to start." I break off a piece of the corn muffin and pop it into my mouth. This seems to satisfy him as he returns his attention to his plate.

When I take a small bite of the rib, I chew rapidly, hoping to avoid tasting the meat, then wash it down with a large drink of iced tea.

There, I did it.

"You need to tell me right now what's going on," Lance suddenly demands.

Shit. I focused so hard on keeping the food down that I didn't notice Lance watching me. He's way too observant for me to keep up this charade any longer.

10

LANCE

"Kellie, I know something is bothering you, so please tell me whatever it is."

"I'm fine, really."

"Is it the investigation?" Of course, everyone responds to traumatic events differently, so I attributed her odd behavior to the stresses of the past few days. But as I continue to read her body language and note the dancing of her eyes, I see the shift. I'm concerned she's keeping something to herself instead of leaning on me for support.

"I don't know what you're talking about." Kellie flashes a forced toothy smile, then takes a tiny bite of the meat and quickly follows it with a sip of her tea. "Quit staring at me and eat your dinner."

"But I like looking at you," I say playfully, hoping to get her to open up, even though she appears lost in thought. Pushing the vegetables around her plate with her fork, she slices a small red potato into quarters. "Are you sure you're feeling okay?"

"I told you, I'm fine." With the side of her fork, she cuts

the potato once more then pops the tiny sliver into her mouth. With a grimace, she swallows. "See, I'm eating."

"That isn't even enough to sustain a chipmunk." Thinking back, I try to remember the last time I saw her consume a full meal. I'm pretty sure it was before we went to the park with Rory. But I can't place when exactly.

"Ha, ha. That's funny...I didn't know you were an expert in what chipmunks ate." Her words are flat and almost monotone. She still avoids my gaze and concentrates on lining up the knife and spoon lying beside her plate.

"Yeah, hilarious," I reply, my tone lacking all humor.

Kellie lifts the rib close to her mouth and tentatively sniffs at it. Her nose wrinkles and she immediately places it back onto her plate uneaten.

"If you don't like the food, I can make you something else." I push my chair back and stand, intending to find something she does want.

"No, sit down, please." She wipes her hands on the cloth napkin, removing the BBQ sauce left on her fingers.

"If it's not the food, then what is it?" She shuffles on her chair but doesn't respond. "I can't help you if you don't tell me what has you so twisted up inside."

"Fine," she mumbles, then reaches under the table. "I'd planned on waiting until after dinner, but here." She hands me a small square gift box that's tied up with a blue and silver ribbon. "This is for you."

"What is it?" Confused, I sit down and push my plate to the center of the table to make room for the box. "My birthday isn't for another month."

"Just open it."

Removing the ribbon, I set it aside and lift the lid. Under several layers of tissue paper, I see what looks like a small white cotton rag. "Should I use this to wash my truck?"

"Look again," she huffs, then slides the gift closer to me.

I tip the box over and the small cloth falls onto the table. It's a tiny T-shirt with the name Malloy printed in blue lettering. *It's too tiny for Rory. Maybe it's for Tigress?* I hold it up and chuckle. "Uh, Kel, I don't think this will fit me." My sense of humor sparks no reaction from her.

"Try looking at the other side," she says quietly, chewing on her thumbnail.

When I turn the shirt over, my gaze settles on the design. More of the same blue lettering surrounds what looks like a deputy badge. I read it to myself several times, letting it sink in.

FUTURE DEPUTY SHERIFF
JUST LIKE MY DADDY

"Are you kidding me?" Little by little, the pieces of the puzzle fall into place. Kellie's lack of appetite and seeing her rush from the dinner table to the bathroom last night with an upset stomach has nothing to do with the concussion. No wonder she's been distracted and in another world.

"I wouldn't lie about this, Lance."

"You're serious?" Shit, I'm screwing this up. Never in a million years did I expect Kellie to drop this on me. The shock finally wears off and my brain engages. "Does this mean what I think it means?"

"That depends. What do you think it means?"

I feel a grin slowly spread across my face as I formulate a plan to make this a moment I'll never forget. Fifty years from now, I want to remember the exact moment Kellie told me I would be a father for the first time.

"Well, Ms. Bryant. Using my expert detective skills, I'd say someone is pregnant."

"What else do these skills tell you?" The twinkle in her

eyes tells me she caught on to my little game and is playing along.

"Using the most sophisticated, hi-tech equipment," I tap my finger on my temple. "It's possible; the daddy-to-be is a deputy." I slide my chair back and pull her onto my lap.

"Very intuitive of you, Deputy Malloy."

"Putting all of these clues together, I conclude you've made me the happiest man alive because we are going to have a beautiful baby."

Kellie's expression softens as the secret she's been holding on to is finally out in the open.

"Are you sure you're ready to be a daddy?"

"Absolutely, positively. There's nothing I want more than to have a family with you." Resting my palm gently on her belly, I lean in and whisper against her lips, "This is the best gift you could have given me. Thank you."

"You're really okay with it." Her eyes light up with anticipation.

"I've never been happier." I reach behind her and grab the T-shirt. Laying it over her flat belly, I imagine how big it will be in a few months.

"I can't wait to tell our parents." Mom and Dad are going to be elated to learn of their first grandchild.

"Um, well, about that." Her nose wrinkles. "My mom walked in on me while I was throwing up and put two and two together. Then she told your mom. I'm surprised you didn't pick up on their hints over dinner."

"Ah, it all makes sense now. I usually have to beg for Mom to cook me her famous baby back ribs."

"I'm sorry, I wanted you to be the first to know, but my mom's intuition was on high alert."

"Well, there's no way my dad doesn't know by now."

"And mine. Oh shit," she gasps.

"What? What's wrong? What hurts?" My hands fly to her stomach.

She tries to stand, but I hold her in place.

"No, sorry. I'm fine. It just dawned on me, if they are talking about the baby in front of Rory, she's going to have a lot of questions."

"There's not much we can do about it tonight."

"You're right, but I didn't plan on telling her right away. I'm worried she's going to be jealous of the baby."

"I'm an only child, so I don't know how that works." Mom said she wanted a house full of children but weren't blessed with more.

"It happens. Mom said Leslie hated me and even put me in a box to send me back to the hospital."

"I guess we need to keep empty boxes away from Rory." I try to sound serious but can't hide my amusement.

"No, that's not what I'm saying." Kellie shoves my shoulder playfully.

"I know. We'll just have to make sure Rory knows how much we love her. That she's just as important as the baby and what a big responsibility it is to be a big sister." I catch myself, but Kellie doesn't correct me. Technically, I know they will be cousins, but it just feels like Rory will be the baby's sister. "I think they will be the best of friends."

"I hope so."

"When is our baby due?"

"The doctor at the hospital said we have about thirty-two weeks to go."

"Okay, so that means he or she will be here in... " I count on my fingers and lose track. My head spins, trying to calculate the days, weeks, and months. *How the hell do they figure this stuff out?*

"It's about seven-ish months," she inserts. "I have an appointment to see my doctor later this week."

"Gotcha." I wrap my arms around Kellie's waist, pulling her snugly against my chest.

We sit in silence as I try to make sense of everything. A baby. Another person for me to love and protect. My number one priority will be keeping them safe and defending my family against Trish or whoever is trying to harm them, no matter the cost.

I've come to terms with Paul's death, but I wish he was still here. This momentous occasion is meant to be shared with my best friend. He and I should be celebrating my becoming a father over a few beers. We had plans to raise our children together, and now my baby will never know what a great man Paul was.

"Are you okay? You went quiet on me." Kellie's voice snaps me back into the moment.

"Yeah, fine. It's just that I can't believe I'm going to be a dad." A lump sits in my throat as I'm overcome with emotions. "I love you so much, Kellie."

She swipes her thumb over my cheek, catching a tear I didn't realize had escaped. "I love you more, Sir Lancelot." She stands and takes my hand, leading me down the hall to her bedroom. "Come with me. I have something else I think you'll like."

"There's more?" I ask, wondering what else she could have up her sleeve. "I can't imagine anything better than you being the mother to my child."

She flashes a wicked smile and opens her bedroom door. The room is bathed in candlelight and rose petals cover the bed. "I'm pretty confident you'll like this surprise too."

Without fail, my internal alarm clock wakes me before the sun rises. No matter how hard I try, it doesn't recognize the rare days I don't work. For too long, I've survived on very little sleep and last night was no different. Only instead of dragging my ass out of bed, I have a burst of energy. My mind is still racing with how to prove Trish is the one who took Rory, but the news of becoming a father has overshadowed it for the time being.

Sure, the baby wasn't planned, but that doesn't mean it's unwanted or will be unloved. For months, I've envisioned a future with Kellie, and although it may seem like our relationship has moved from zero to a hundred, when it's meant to be, fighting it is a waste of time.

Listening to the guys at work talk about their girlfriends makes me realize how good I have it. If I believed the crap they spread around the locker room, my way of thinking means I'm pussy whipped. I suppose to them it's all mushy stuff that women dream of, and guys like to pretend doesn't matter. I was just like them at one time but meeting Kellie has changed how I view relationships.

Little do they realize, falling in love with your soulmate isn't planned, but destiny. I watched it happen to Paul and Jane but never thought I'd be fortunate enough to find it myself.

Meeting the person you can't live without is like being buried under a ton of bricks. The weight of it is too much for you to handle alone. But you don't have to because the one you love is there to help you climb out from under the rubble. At least that's how it feels for me.

Kellie has stood beside me through good times and bad. She's seen me broken from heartache and fear. Last night the past finally faded away and I cried tears of joy with the knowledge that we will be adding to our family.

Pulling Kellie close to my body, I look down at her snuggled in my arms. With my constantly changing work hours, quiet moments like this are few and far between. No doubt, these lazy mornings will disappear once the baby arrives.

I've never been happier than I am right now. My world revolves around keeping my family safe. It's my responsibility to provide a good life for them and be the best dad I can be. Once Kellie agrees to marry me, everything will fall into place, and my life will be complete.

But, along with joy comes the fear that it could be taken away in the blink of an eye. So, I need to treasure every moment. Enjoy life to its fullest. And most importantly, I need to remember to never let a day go by without telling my family how much they are loved.

"Lance... baby..." Kellie mumbles and rolls back to her side of the bed, taking all the blankets with her. I guess that's my signal to get up.

Since Kellie didn't eat more than a few potatoes last night, I plan to have breakfast ready before she wakes. The instant my feet hit the floor, Kellie stretches her arms and legs, repositioning herself like a starfish across the entire mattress.

"Bed hog," I grumble and shake my head. But I'm not bothered by it. Kellie can have every inch of the bed if it means she gets the rest she needs.

Digging through my bag, I find a clean pair of sweats and a T-shirt to put on before going to the kitchen. Kellie mentioned that so far, it's more the smell of food that makes her nauseous, so I decided on something bland, like scrambled eggs and toast.

Preoccupied with the breakfast menu, I step into the hall and nearly trip over Tigress. "Damn it, cat, move." I slide my foot gently under her butt to scoot her away, but she doesn't budge. "Are you really this lazy?" I must be tired if I'm talking to the cat and expecting her to reply. Tigress doesn't move but hisses at me before going back to cleaning her paws. "So sorry, your royal highness. I'll just step around you."

Before I reach the kitchen door, the smell of food cooking hits me.

"Lance, is that you?" My mother's voice floats from the kitchen.

I should have known they would be here already, but I'm surprised and a little pissed with myself that I didn't hear anybody enter the house. I step into the kitchen. "Uh, yeah. Unless you know of some other man that would be here at this hour."

"Smarty-pants." She flicks a dishtowel in my direction. "Sit down."

"What are you doing here so early?"

"We thought we'd pop over and get things started, let you and Kellie sleep in."

The kitchen is bustling. By the looks of it, Mom and Angie have cooked enough to feed a small army. Tom, Rory, and my dad are seated at the table, eating a feast of potatoes, eggs, pancakes, and bacon.

"Good morning." Angie greets me while handing me a cup of coffee.

"Morning," I reply and take a sip. "Thank you."

"Help yourself to a plate."

"Coffee is great for now. I'll wait until Kellie gets up before I eat." I sit down beside Rory, who is making a mess eating pancakes swimming in syrup.

"Hi, Lance," Rory says between bites. "Where's Addy K?"

"Hey, princess. She's still sleeping. Did you have a good night at Gram Gram's?"

"Yep. Guess what?"

"Tell me."

"Helen made me a special chocolate banana milkshake."

"That's awesome. Did you save me any?"

"No." She rolls her eyes and throws her hands up in the air. "It would melt."

"That's true. Maybe we can go again soon so I can get my own milkshake."

"Yes!" She shrieks and holds her fork up triumphantly, which causes syrup to drip down her arm.

"Whoa. Slow down." I take the fork from her and place it on her plate. "Mom, can you get me a wet towel?"

"Here you go." Using the rag she tossed to me, I wipe up the sticky mess.

"She eats like you used to," Mom says, taking the towel from me.

"You mean like he still does," Dad chimes in.

"Hey, when did it become pick on Lance day?" I clutch my chest as if I've been wounded. "Rory, save me."

She puts her hands on her hips. "Be nice, Grumpa David or Mr. Deputy Bear will arrest you."

"Whatever you say, Rory." He plays along. "I don't want to be arrested, not before I've eaten breakfast anyway."

"Yeah, Dad. Be nice to me." Rory climbs onto my lap and wraps her arms around my neck protectively. A year ago, I'd never have imagined having a little girl I adore, a girlfriend I hope to marry, and a baby on the way.

"Soooo," Mom says, sliding up beside me. "How was dinner last night?"

I know she's hoping I'll mention the baby, but the devil in me wants to see how long I can keep quiet and make them carry on with their pretenses.

"It was delicious. Thanks for cooking." I rub my stomach for effect.

"Oh, it was no trouble at all. Did you like the *baby* back ribs?" Mom emphasizes the word baby.

"Oh yes, they were great." I hide my smile behind my coffee mug. "I put the leftovers in the fridge."

"I'll take some. She wouldn't let me have any last night." Dad grumbles.

"Mom made a ton, so there's plenty for everyone to have some for lunch."

"So, it was just a quiet night then. Nothing unusual?" Angie asks, fishing for information I'm not ready to share.

"Oh, there was one thing we talked about," I say casually.

"What thing?" Mom perks up. She and Angie are practically vibrating with excitement. I should feel guilty playing this game, but I can't stop now. It's just too bad Kellie isn't here to watch them squirm.

Stalling, I steal a piece of bacon from Rory's plate.

"Hey, that's my bacon," she giggles and snatches it back, taking a big bite.

"Sharing is caring, remember?" I tease and take another piece from the platter in the middle of the table.

"Go on. You were saying," Mom encourages me to continue.

"Oh yeah, Kellie and I..." I pause to take a slow sip of coffee.

"You and Kellie what?" Angie impatiently blurts out.

"Well, let's see. How do I say this? We are going to..." I take a deep breath. "Work in the garden today."

"Oh," Mom and Angie look deflated. "But nothing else?"

"Nothing important. Was there something she should have told me?"

"Oh, for God's sake, woman," Dad snaps. "It's obvious he knows and is just screwing with both of you."

"Oh, you're such a terrible son." Mom smacks my arm, and I can't hold back my laughter. "You're evil, just like your dad."

"Oh, come on. It was fun watching you two suffer." I throw my head back and howl with laughter. "You should have seen your faces."

"Would you believe we weren't even out of the driveway before Tracy told David and me?" Tom rats my mom out.

"Speaking of letting others know about the B-A-B-Y. Kellie and I talked about when and how to tell this little one," I point to Rory, "about the impending arrival. How much did you say around her last night?"

"She may have heard the B-A-B-Y word tossed around a few times," Angie confesses.

"Did you tell her about K-E-L-L-I-E and the B-A-B-Y?" This spelling each word so Rory doesn't understand is going to get old and fast.

"No, of course not." Mom replies.

I'm relieved. "Good. We need to be careful until Kellie gives us the okay to say anything." I level both moms with a stare I hope will keep them quiet.

"We promise to keep the−" Rory interrupts mom.

"B-A-B-Y," Rory repeats.

"Shit, I mean shoot," I stumble over my words.

"That's really good, honey. What do you think that spells?" Angie asks while we all hold our breaths.

"Puppy," she shouts proudly.

We breathe a collective sigh then laughter erupts, filling the room with a feeling of joy. Rory adds her giggles to the mix even though she has no clue why we're all so happy.

"Sounds like a party in here." All eyes turn to Kellie as she walks into the kitchen.

"Morning, Addy K," Rory runs to Kellie, latching onto her legs for dear life.

My heart skips and I can't stop looking at her. Even with messy hair, no makeup, and draped in a ratty old robe, she's the most beautiful woman in the world.

"Congratulations, honey." Mom rushes toward Kellie and hugs her tight. "Your mom said you've been pretty sick. How are you feeling?"

"So far, so good." My eyes travel to where her hand lays protectively over her belly. "Not as queasy as yesterday."

"I vomited for the entire nine months. They even hospitalized me at one point for dehydration." Mom extricates Rory from Kellie's legs, carrying her back to the table.

Kellie's eyes widen.

"Tracy," Angie shoots Mom a worried look. She pulls out a chair beside me for Kellie to sit on. "Don't worry, honey. It does happen, but I'm sure you'll be just fine."

"I'm sorry. I shouldn't have said that." My mom's off-handed remark was just a minor slip-up but could have gone bad quickly.

"It's okay. I know you didn't mean anything by it." Kellie reassures my mom.

Our dads both stand to hug Kellie before leaving to work in the garage. Angie gave Tom a long list of repairs that need doing around the house. My mom volunteered my dad to help. I'm sure it's a ploy to keep the men out of their hair.

"Hey, beautiful." She blushes when I lean in and brush my lips over hers. Kellie's still a little shy when it comes to public displays of affection, but since I don't see myself stopping any time soon, she'll have to get used to it.

"Mom, that's too much food." Angie places a stack of pancakes in front of Kellie.

"Just try a few bites then." I'm worried about her not eating.

"I'll give it a shot." She takes a small bite from the plain pancake. When her face doesn't twist up in disgust, I take it as a good sign she'll be able to keep it down.

"Addy K. I want on your lap." Rory tries climbing over me.

"Hang on a minute." I catch her before she falls. "Addy K needs to eat, and you still need to get dressed."

"But I want Addy K." She pouts. It's not one of her usual; I want my way expressions. I'm worried that spending the night away from Kellie last night may have been too soon.

"Tell you what. Let's switch seats." I stand up and place her in my chair. "You can sit here next to Auntie Kellie, and I'll move to your spot. Does that work?"

Rory nods, but her frown remains firmly in place. I'm not convinced she's entirely in agreement. Climbing down from the chair, she scoots it closer to Kellie. "That's better." This little girl is a problem solver and will get far in life.

"What do you say to Lance?" Kellie gently reminds Rory.

"Thank you, Lance." She leans towards Kellie, as close as possible, without sitting in her lap.

"You're very welcome, sweetheart."

"You're getting good at this parenting thing. I have no doubt you'll be a pro by the time this little one makes his or her arrival." Kellie's compliment fills me with pride.

"With the two of you by my side, there's a good chance I'll be able to make that come true."

Both Kellie and Rory beam up at me making me feel invincible. The only thing that could make my world any better is if Kellie agrees to be my wife.

"Dispatch, show me on office detail at 1032 Distal Road," I call into the station to be taken out of service so I can finish writing reports while sitting in my squad car.

Today is Rory's first day back at school. I offered to take the morning off to be there, but Kellie insisted on doing it alone. So instead of arguing my point, I rearranged my patrol schedule, allowing me to be close by without her knowing. I purposely chose this location for its unobstructed view of the school.

"10-4, Deputy Malloy." The male dispatcher replies, giving me the okay to get caught up on my paperwork while parked. It means I'm only required to answer emergency calls.

Unscrewing the lid on my second energy drink, I down it quickly, hoping to avoid the disgusting liquid from hitting my tongue. I've never liked the taste, but it does the job of keeping me awake while on patrol after a sleepless night.

I spent most of the night mentally ticking off any possible loopholes in the safety protocols at Rory's preschool. After speaking with the director, I was reasonably confident she would be safe, but my trust isn't easily won. Learning they've recently upgraded the entire security system and added more cameras was a relief. However, it didn't take away all of my worries.

Pulling up the report on the computer mounted inside the cruiser, I read the top line three times but didn't comprehend any of it. Too distracted to continue, I close the laptop and stare out the front window.

I sit up straight when Kellie turns the corner and pulls up into the preschool parking lot. As she walks around the front of her car to Rory's side, she scans the area. I'm glad to see she listened when I spoke to her about being more aware of her surroundings.

Rory looks adorable in her new purple dress. Her brunette curls bounce as she skips beside Kellie, eager to return to school. Kellie's wearing a long T-shirt and yoga pants with her hair pulled back into a ponytail. Even from this distance, I can see she's not feeling her best. I'm guessing another morning of vomiting.

I make a mental note to pick up some things I hope will help with her morning sickness. I'll grab something for dinner too so she doesn't have to cook.

When a car alarm blares, Kellie shrieks then pulls Rory protectively into her arms.

Damn it. Maybe I took my warnings too far. I want Kellie to be vigilant but not afraid of her own shadow.

It takes everything I have to stop myself from sprinting over to them. Kellie gathers herself and leads Rory into the school.

The minutes tick by as I wait for Kellie to exit the building. Tapping my thumbs on the steering wheel, I glance at my watch. It's been more than ten minutes and Kellie still hasn't emerged from the school. It shouldn't be taking this long.

During our meeting with the director, she suggested today's drop-off be quick. In her experience, drawing out the goodbye with lots of extra kisses and hugs might upset Rory. So, either Kellie is having difficulty leaving, or Rory is struggling. Either way, my instinct is to rush in and pick up the pieces.

Five more minutes pass and the uneasy feeling in my gut has only gotten worse. Grabbing my phone from the passenger seat, I shoot a text to Kellie.

Lance: Good morning. Did Rory get to school okay?

Impatiently I wait for her reply. "Finally," I huff out. Relief washes over me when I see Kellie leaving the school. She removes her phone from her back pocket and appears to be reading my message.

Kellie: Yeah, she was happy to see her friends.

Lance: That's good. How are you doing?

Her shoulders slump and her feet shuffle along the walkway as she makes her way back to her car. I knew today would be difficult, but I never expected to see her this upset.

Kellie: I'm fine.

Her body language tells me she's anything but fine. She looks up to the sky and appears to say something before continuing towards the parking lot. Sliding into the driver's seat, she holds onto the steering wheel. Even from a few yards away, I can see her shoulders shake as she sobs.

Reaching for the switch, I flip on my lights to draw attention to where I'm parked.

Lance: Kellie. Look over to your right.

Using the long sleeve on her shirt, she wipes at her cheeks. She reads her phone and turns her head in my direction.

Shutting off the lights, I drive over to be near her. I park alongside her car, allowing us to chat through open driver's side windows without getting out of our vehicles.

Her eyes are red, and her cheeks tear stained.

"Hey, babe." I reach into my pocket and offer her a handkerchief.

"Thanks, but I've got one already." She removes it from her purse and dabs at the corners of her eyes. "An extraordinary man gave it to me."

"Are you mad at me for showing up?"

"No, I'm glad you came. I was sure I could do it alone but letting go of Rory's hand today brought back every memory from the park." She covers her face, trying to hide her pain.

Exiting my car, I open her door. "Come here." Helping her from the driver's seat. I pull her into my arms and whisper, "I'll always be here for you, Rory, and our baby."

I never want her to feel like she needs to be alone again. The engagement ring is at home, but everything in me says it's the right time to ask her to be my wife.

"Kellie, I love you. You're the strongest woman I know." I hold her away from my body so I can see her eyes.

"I love you too," she sniffs.

"Dispatch to Deputy Malloy. What's your location?" Before I can recite my rehearsed proposal, my radio goes off.

"Fuck," I mutter my frustration then speak into the mic on my shoulder. "10-7. Out of service for office detail at 1032 Distal Road." I reply and wait for dispatch to respond.

"10-4, Deputy Malloy. Lieutenant Cartwright requests you to 10-19."

"10-4 ETA is ten minutes."

"What does all of that mean?" Her brows pinch with confusion.

"10-19 is code for I need to return to the station immediately. I'm sorry, I'll explain more later. I have to go. Will you be okay?" Every part of me wants to stay, but I don't have a choice. It's not an emergency situation, but it's still urgent, and I need to get there fast.

"Yeah, I'm good. Go do your cop stuff and save the world." She stands on tiptoes and kisses my lips quickly. "I love you. Be safe."

"I love you more."

Jumping in my car, I hit the lights and sirens. I was so close, but as usual, just as I am ready to ask the most important question of my life, duty calls and delays me once more.

11

KELLIE

"Let's go over them one more time. What does 10-4 mean?" While we lay in bed, Lance continues to test me on the Sheriff's Department radio codes. My question about how he communicates with dispatch turned into a study session that seemingly has no end in sight.

"10-4 is how you reply to another person, so they know–" a huge yawn cuts my sentence short.

"Good enough." Laying on his side, he props himself up on his elbow and uses his fingertip to lightly draw circles on my arm.

"Before I forget, Mom asked me to remind you about dinner on Wednesday. Do you still have the night off?"

"Yep, cleared it with Sarge already."

"Great, we need to be there by 6pm." I won't be surprised if things change before then, but I am learning to roll with it.

"Since we're talking about schedules," he pauses. "I'll be late getting home tomorrow night."

"Oh?"

"I'm going to a peer meeting with Jackson."

"Thanks for letting me know." I keep my tone neutral.

Outwardly, I don't want to make a big deal about his meeting, but on the inside, I'm celebrating his ongoing commitment to himself.

"Alright. Now that our schedules are synched let's get back to business—10-9?"

"You really are having fun, aren't you?"

"More than you know." Lance walks his fingers down to the top of my thigh, eliciting a wave of goosebumps.

"Why are you so intent on me getting these memorized?"

"I don't always have time to chat while at work. I thought it could be a fun and quick way to text each other."

"I'll never remember all of them."

"That's why we're practicing. I'll even make you a cheat sheet."

"That will help," I reply, trying to sound interested and supportive.

"You can do it. 10-9, what's it mean?"

"Repeat the last transmission," I say proudly, knowing I nailed it.

"You can do it. 10-9, what's it mean?" he repeats the same question, cracking up at his own joke.

"Smartass. I see you've been practicing Dad jokes. You'll be a social media superstar before you know it." I push his hand away from my thigh and kick off the heavy duvet. "Time for bed. We both have to work tomorrow. I don't want to look like a zombie when I take Rory to school in the morning."

"Okay, but just one more. 10-35."

"Nope. I'm going to sleep. Good night," I whisper, then kiss his cheek.

"Sweet dreams." Lance lays back on his pillow and is finally quiet.

Closing my eyes, I concentrate on slowing my breathing,

hoping it will help me relax and shut off my brain. As I drift off, Lance's husky voice jolts me awake.

"Kellie, are you asleep?"

"Yes." I tug hard on the top sheet and wrap my legs around it so he can't have any. "Now leave me alone and let me sleep."

"Come on. If you get this code right, I promise you'll be handsomely rewarded."

Figuring it best to ignore him, I don't answer. Just when I think I've won, Lance pokes my arm.

"Um, Kellie. Did you go back to sleep?"

I open one eyelid and see him smiling down on me. "You're not going to shut up until I give you an answer, are you?"

"Nope."

"Fine, you win. But when I'm cranky tomorrow, you'll wish you'd let me sleep." I blow out an exasperated breath and make my best guess, praying I'm right so we can end this silly game. "Does it mean that you've arrived on the scene?"

"No, sorry, that would be 10-97." He sits up and turns to face me. For some unknown reason, these lessons seem to be very important to him. "Think of 10-97 as ninety-seven people, showing up at your house. They've arrived on the scene. Get it?"

"Sure. Whatever you say. Can we be done now?"

Seemingly unaware of my mounting frustration and need for sleep, he keeps going.

"To remember 10-35, I go back to my academy days. We had thirty-six recruits in my class. Me and thirty-five partners. They were the ones I depended on for help." My eyelids are just slits as he continues to drone on. "Hey, are you listening?"

"I'm awake. You said, thirty-five partners." I snap my eyes open and blink a few times to focus on his face.

"So, if I need backup, I would call for my thirty-five part-ners. Therefore, 10-35 is a request for help or backup. This one is important to remember."

"Hmmm, yeah. Super important. Yep."

He continues talking, but in my state of exhaustion, all I can focus on is the handsome man beside me. The moonlight reflects in his eyes, making them appear grey while other times they seem blue. Either way, he is the most attractive man I've ever met.

Existing somewhere between awake and asleep, my imag-ination starts to run wild. Memories of the last time we made love flash through my mind. It has me fully aroused and half tempted to straddle his hips.

While Lance rambles on about numbers and why they are important, I consider my options. Sleep or a hot night of sex? The answer is obvious. I'm wiped out. Sleep is the big winner tonight, but maybe I'll be raring to go tomorrow, that's if I get some rest.

"Kellie, if you keep staring at me like that, you won't be getting any sleep tonight." A fire burns behind Lance's eyes as they wander over my body.

"If you hadn't wasted so much time testing me on codes, I wouldn't be so worn out, and we could do something about it. Instead, you drained all my energy, so I'll have to give you a raincheck."

"That's just mean." He puts on a sad face.

"I'm sorry to disappoint you. Growing this baby is already wearing me out. On top of wanting to sleep all the time, I'm bloated, my boobs hurt, and I saw a gigantic zit on my nose this morning." My mood swings have ridden the border between temper tantrums and floating on cloud nine.

"Is all of that normal?" His tone holds a hint of fear.

"According to the multiple pregnancy books I've down-loaded, it's normal. Oh, and don't even get me started on the horrifying gas I've had all day." I'm a little embarrassed about that last part, but he should experience the wide range of pregnancy symptoms alongside me.

He covers his mouth to stifle his laughter which only serves to aggravate me.

"It's not funny, jerk." I turn my back to him and switch off the bedside lamp.

"I'm sorry. I wasn't making fun of you." Lance scoots closer and places a kiss on my shoulder. "I didn't mean to upset you."

"Deep down, I know, but tell that to my hormones. They're the ones in charge now." My eyes well up with tears. These emotional ups and downs are another not so fun part of pregnancy I hope will soon pass.

"Sweetheart, don't cry." He gently tugs on my shoulder and rolls me onto my side to face him. "You are beautiful, sexy, and perfect."

"You won't say that when I look like a penguin wearing a mu-mu, smuggling a beach ball into the movies." I shove a pillow under my shirt to make my point.

Lance's face turns beet red while he holds his breath, attempting to stay in control.

"Go ahead. Let it out before you explode." I give him permission to laugh because this visual is pretty funny.

"Yeah, even then, you'd be the most gorgeous woman at the theater. And just think, you'll be able to sneak in all the candy we can eat." He leans over and blows a raspberry on my tummy. There's no bump yet, but Lance still likes to talk to the baby, which I find adorable. He's going to be the most amazing Dad. "What do you think, kiddo? Is your mommy the prettiest woman in the world?"

He turns his head like he's listening to the baby's response. "Yeah, and what else?"

"You are ridiculous." His short hair tickles my belly while

he pretends to have an entire conversation with his unborn child.

"So, we both agree," he says with a smirk.

"Of course, the little princess agrees with her Daddy?" I raise a brow waiting for what I know is coming next.

"You mispronounced it again. It's prince. No *ss* on the end." Lance insists the baby is a boy and I just like to mess with him.

"Anyway, our baby, boy or girl, doesn't have to see your face to know how beautiful you are."

He must have lost his mind.

"Did you just roll your eyes at me, Ms. Bryant?" Lance lifts the back of my hand to his lips, placing kisses on each knuckle. "It's true, you know. Our baby is the only person who can honestly say how pure your heart is because he's the only one to hear it beat from the inside."

"Way to make the pregnant woman cry again with your poetic words," I whimper through a giggle. "You must have read that somewhere."

"Busted, but I think I mixed up the words." He kisses the tears on my cheeks before placing his lips on mine.

"Maybe, but it did the trick. Thank you."

"Nothing will ever stop me from loving every inch of you."

"I love you more." I cup his cheek and kiss him chastely, then snuggle under the blankets.

"Uh, Kel?"

"What?"

"You haven't answered the last question."

"I may kill you, Deputy. What question would that be?"

"10-35," he says sheepishly.

"Do you promise it will be the last one?" My vision has begun to blur from lack of sleep.

"For tonight, yes."

"Fine. 10-35 is a when I need back up from your thirty-five partners."

"Perfect. And now for the bonus round..." He wears a sexy smile like it will shield him from my wrath.

"You've got to be kidding me. You said that was the last question." "I know, but this is just a refresher. For an extra ten points, tell me again what 10-97 means?" He hums the theme from Jeopardy.

"Fine! Ninety-seven people are going to show up at my house."

"You are correct!" His enthusiasm is not shared by me. "You win the bonus round! Tell her what she's won, Bob."

"It better be an awesome prize."

"Roll over and I'll rub your back until you go to sleep."

"10-4, Deputy Malloy. I love your version of 10-35. But understand, you'll need to 10-9 this massage every night from now on."

～

The sun is still low when I'm woken by Lance exploring my body with light caresses.

"What time is it?" I ask, feeling sleep deprived and very aroused from his touch and the sexy dreams I've had all night.

"It's still early." His teeth scrape my shoulder and I melt into him. "I couldn't sleep."

"Lance," I moan as his mouth moves over the slope of my neck. Turning sleepily onto my back, I stare deep into his eyes. His pupils are dark with desire, surely matching my own.

With strong but gentle hands, he frames my face then brushes his lips over mine. His kisses are slow and sensual, sending a wave of goosebumps over my body.

"You're so beautiful. How did I get this lucky?"

"I could ask the same thing about you." Pulling his mouth down to mine, I take control, pouring all my love into this moment. A lifetime of his kisses will never be enough for me.

"You won't be needing this." Lance eases my shirt over my head, tossing it to the floor.

Leaning in, he places tender kisses on the swells of my breasts. Greedily, I thrust my chest into his hands. I moan my pleasure as Lance closes his mouth over one nipple while working the other one between his fingers. I've never been this on fire before.

Hungry for more, I place my hands on his shoulders and urge him to go lower.

His muscles tense under my fingers. "Just as impatient as ever," he laughs with a glint of humor in his eyes.

"You are still infuriatingly slow, Deputy." I fall back against my pillow and exhale a ragged breath.

"I've told you before, good things come to those who wait." He chuckles and brushes his lips below my belly button. The stubble of his unshaven jaw scrapes against my skin when finally he settles between my thighs.

A soft moan escapes from my lips as he slides one finger inside me and then another. All the tension and stress I've been hanging onto for days is wiped away in an instant.

"Holy shit." My body vibrates with excitement. Teetering on the brink, I arch into him as the sensation builds within my core. Another swipe of his talented tongue and my world spins out of control as an intense orgasm rips through me.

Eyes squeezed tight, I continue to rock against his hand until the pulses slow and my breathing returns to normal. Finally, I fall back and sink into the mattress, luxuriating in the sweet sensations rolling through me.

"You are very good at that," I say, breathless and zapped of all energy. His cocky grin and swagger are well earned tonight.

"We aren't done yet, sweetheart."

His throaty growl vibrates in his chest as he moves up my body, settling his weight over me. Our eyes remain locked as he slides inside, filling me completely. He pauses before easing himself back out, then in slowly. Each thrust is unhurried and steady as he makes love to me.

Moving as one, I lift my hips to meet his gentle strokes and bury my face into the curve of his neck to quiet my cries of pleasure. I clench my muscles, gripping his cock as another orgasm tears through me.

Lance's pace increases as he seeks his own release. His breathing grows ragged, and in an instant, the gentle lover from earlier has disappeared. He hammers into me repeatedly before sending himself over the edge.

He collapses on top of me, breathless and satisfied. Rolling off me, he pulls me against his side. I close my eyes, loving the feel of his fingertips running up and down my spine. "I love you, Lance." Never have I felt so loved and protected as I do now, wrapped up in the warmth of Lance's arms. Our lives may not be perfect, but it is close enough for me, and that's all that matters.

With my head laying on Lance's shoulder and just before sleep overtakes me, I hear him whisper, "You are part of everything good in my world and I never want to live another day without you by my side."

Rolling over in bed, I reach for Lance, but he's not there. He doesn't work until this afternoon, so I'm surprised to feel his side of the bed is cold. I don't remember falling back to sleep after our early morning of lovemaking. The ache between my thighs will stay with me all day as a reminder of what Lance and I shared.

Rather than jumping out of bed and starting the day off with a puking session, I follow Mom's suggestions. I sit up slowly and lay back against the headboard, munching on plain saltine crackers and taking small sips of warm ginger ale. To be honest, it's pretty disgusting but seems to be working. The only downside is having cracker crumbs in our bed. The tradeoff between throwing up and shaking out the blankets before we go to sleep is well worth it.

The alarm on my phone goes off an hour earlier than usual so I can get a few things done before taking Rory to school. Slowly climbing out of bed, I'm excited when I'm able to stand without feeling any queasiness. I turn off the alarm, scroll through my playlist, and select a song that matches my mood. Finding the perfect one, I press play and sing along as Louis Armstrong's *What a Wonderful World* serenades me while going about my morning routine.

Before I can jump into the shower, I hear male voices coming from down the hall in what sounds like a heated discussion. I'm sure one of them is Lance's. His voice is raised to a level I'm afraid will wake and scare Rory.

"What the fuck do you expect from me, Jackson? I just found out I have a baby on the way."

I hurry to throw on some clothes, nearly falling face first when I trip over Lance's boots.

"Just don't be stupid and do something you might regret later." The other man says even louder.

Rushing into the living room, I stop dead when I see Lance nose to nose with Jackson. "Hey! What are you two yelling about?"

Jackson shoves Lance away from him and turns to look at me. He schools his features before speaking. "I'm sorry, Kellie. We didn't mean to wake you."

"You didn't, but with your shouting, I'm surprised you didn't wake Rory."

"Sorry, Babe," Lance walks over to me and leans down to kiss my cheek, but I step away. Something doesn't feel right about this situation. "Jackson and I were just having a difference of opinion about an arrest he needs to make."

"Are you sure that's all it was? You seemed so angry."

"It happens sometimes. I was just venting my frustration over some work stuff," Jackson says calmly.

"Yeah, you should have heard Paul and me. We used to get into some colossal arguments that would wake the dead." Lance stops abruptly, no doubt catching his bad choice of words. "Well, you know what I mean."

My heart sinks when he mentions Paul. Knowing he was the one who Lance shared everything with, it only makes sense that Jackson would have stepped in and become his sounding board.

"I better get going. Sarge will want an update." Jackson gives me a friendly hug.

"I'll catch up with you tonight so we can finish this conversation." Lance claps Jackson's shoulder. "We can't afford to get this wrong."

"I know." Jackson pauses before walking out the door and turns back to address me. "Sorry again for being so loud."

"No worries. See you soon. Be safe."

As Jackson closes the door, Rory runs down the hall with her blanket dragging behind her.

"Good morning, sweetheart." Lance lifts her into his arms like she weighs nothing.

"Morning," she mumbles into his shoulder.

"Hey, sleepy girl." I rub her back. "Did we wake you up?"

She nods and pops her thumb into her mouth.

"I'm sorry. Tell you what," Lance begins. "How about my two favorite girls climb back into bed for a morning nap, and

I'll make breakfast?" Rory lifts her head off his shoulder. "What would you like me to make?"

"Pancakes?"

"If that's what you want." Lance has a look in his eyes that I've come to recognize well. Rory could ask him for anything right now and he wouldn't say no.

"And sausage?" She asks in a squeaky voice.

"Whatever you want, kiddo." With Rory on his hip, he clasps my hand in his. "And what does Auntie Kellie want?"

I wrap my arms around both of them and squeeze tight. I'm not sure my life can be any better. "Nothing, because everything I want is right here beside me."

Before pulling out of the driveway to take Rory to school, I decide it's time to call Gina and let her know about the baby.

I pop in the new *AirPods* I bought instead of using the car speaker, hoping to keep Rory from hearing anymore baby talk. This means I'll need to be very creative about telling her because even spelling the word baby gets her attention. Although she's convinced it spells puppy and since she asked Lance, I expect him to show up with one any day now.

I pull up Gina's number and press call.

"Good morning." She answers, sounding cheerier than I feel. "How is my best friend and my perfect little angel doing today?"

"You wouldn't call her that if you saw what a terror she's been this morning."

"Oh, no. What happened?"

"Lance was supposed to be watching her while I was in the shower. But when he was cleaning up the breakfast dishes, she got into my makeup bag and painted herself up to look like a clown."

"Please tell me you took pictures." She laughs, seeing the brighter side of the mess I had to clean up.

"Of course I did. It's blackmail for when she's a teenager."

"Evil, but it just might work."

"Oh, but that's not all. She twisted the round brush in her hair, tangling it so bad I had to snip some of her curls. When I tried to fix it, I ended up cutting too much and now it's shorter on the left side of her head."

"You didn't." Gina gasps. "Her hair was finally long enough for a ponytail instead of those two short stubs sticking out of the sides of her head."

"I know, but I had to do it, or she would be walking around with a brush hanging off the side of her head." I glance back at Rory who is quietly watching a movie on her tablet. "Shoot, I'm almost at the preschool, but there's one more thing I need to share with you."

"There's more? Wow, you really have had an eventful morning. Let's hear it so you can get it off your chest."

"Funny you should mention my chest." Just the opening I was looking for to tell her about the baby. "After all of that, I spilled a big cup of decaf coffee on my shirt. It soaked through to the only bra that still fits."

"Why would you be drinking decaf? I thought only pregnant women and old people drink that stuff." I can practically see her scratching her head. "And why don't your bras fit?"

"Umm, because my boobs are growing faster than my belly." I wait a minute to let Gina replay that sentence in her head.

"Holy shit! No way! You're pregnant!"

"Stop yelling. You're going to make me deaf."

"Okay, I'm calm now. Are you really pregnant?"

"Yes, and before you ask, I'm not certain on my due date yet. I still need to see my doctor."

"I'm so excited Kellie. You and Lance are perfect together."

"I think so too. Now it's your turn. Maybe we can have our kids together if you and Dirk hurry up."

"Well, it's not for lack of trying." If Gina had her way, they would have had a honeymoon baby.

"I gotta go. I'll call you later." I turn off the ignition and lean back in my seat.

"Sounds good and Kel," she sniffles and based on the cracking of her voice, I'd bet she's got tears in her eyes. But she's always been a softie. "I'm so happy for you and Lance. You both deserve some happy times."

"Thanks, Gina." I disconnect the call and look at Rory in my review mirror. "Put your *iPad* down. I'll come around to get you."

Walking around the car, I scan the area carefully, just as Lance taught me. There are a few cars around that I recognize as belonging to other parents. Actually, the lot is emptier than usual, but there's nothing strange that I can see.

Opening the side door, Rory shouts, "It's my birthday!"

"No, your birthday isn't for another week," I correct her.

"But Ms. Giulia said it's my turn for the birthday crown." She sounds confused and a little sad.

"Oh, that's right. It is your big day at school." Damn it. I forgot to bring the cupcakes. I'll need to run to the bakery and get back here early for pick up so Rory can hand them out to her friends after school.

"I like Ms. Giulia. She's nice." Rory links her fingers in mine and swings our hands back and forth. Ms. Giulia is the new teacher that Rory can't stop talking about. She took over from Ms. Emma, who's out on maternity leave.

Walking into the building, Rory shrugs out of her jacket, leaving it on the floor at my feet. "There's Carl!" Rory sprints away from me to play blocks with her friend and after the morning I had, I didn't try to stop her.

"Hi, Kellie." Carl's mom is busy placing items into his cubby. We've run into each other a few times but don't discuss the day at the park.

"Good morning."

"Hey!"

"Those two are very cute together."

"I think my son has a crush on Rory." She bumps my shoulder playfully.

"Ha! Don't let Lance hear that. He's already drawn up plans to build a tower in the backyard to keep the boys at bay."

I fold Rory's jacket intending to place it inside her cubby when I see a gift bag with sparkles and pink tissue paper poking out the top.

"Is this from Carl?"

"No. I don't know where that came from. I saw it there when I was putting his lunchbox away."

"Maybe it's something they do for all the kids on their special day to wear the birthday crown."

"I don't think so. Carl's birthday was last month, and he didn't get anything."

"Rory, come here." She and Carl walk over to stand in front of me.

"You have a present." I take the card out of the bag and show it to her. "It says Happy Birthday, Rory."

I hand it to her while I open the card. Carl and Rory giggle and rip the bag apart like wild animals fighting over a bone.

The front of the card is simple. Balloons spell out Happy Birthday. Inside I find a picture of Lance and me standing beside his squad car. I recognize it from Rory's first day back at school. It's covered in dark red spots that look like blood drops and my face has been scratched out with something sharp.

"What the hell is this?" I mumble to myself.

Blood drains from my cheeks when I see the next picture. It's of Rory running through the school playground in the same dress she wore yesterday. Turning it over, my heart stops beating. Scribbled on the back is a note. "I WON'T FAIL TWICE."

"Look, Addy K. A new bunny!" Rory squeals excitedly, hugging the same kind of stuffed bunny my mom was still trying to repair.

Feet rooted to the floor, I watch Rory run off to play with her friends. My body trembles and I feel sick to my stomach. The pieces of the puzzle all begin to fall into place. *It has to be Trish who took Rory.*

"Kellie?" A hand touches my shoulder and I spin around ready to fight. It's Ms. Giulia. "Is everything alright?"

"Where did this bag come from?" My tone is short and sharp.

"I placed it there this morning," she says cheerfully like she's done nothing wrong.

"You what?" I shout. The room falls silent, and a few kids rush over to their parents. They glare at me for upsetting their children, but I can't find it in me to care.

"I-I d-don't understand. R-Rory's Auntie Trish asked me to make sure she got it," she stutters. "She said it was a surprise for her birthday."

"Get Mrs. Warner in here right now," I demand.

"Of course." Visibly shaken, she rushes down the hall to the director's office.

I pull my phone from my purse and scroll to find Lance's number.

"Good morning, Beautiful."

I try to speak, but the air has been squeezed from

my lungs.

"Kellie, are you there?"

"Lance…" I gasp.

"Kellie, what's wrong? Is it the baby?"

"I need you…" is all I can manage to say before the dam bursts releasing an uncontrollable flood of tears.

"Where are you?"

"Rory's school." The room spins as the sounds of children playing fade away. "It was Trish…" My shoulders sag and I choke back the sobs threatening to rip through me.

"Fuck! I'm on my way." Sirens blare in the background and his engine revs.

The line goes dead. My arms fall to my sides and the phone slips from my fingers to the floor. I tell myself to be calm that Lance is coming, and he'll protect Rory and me just as he promised. He won't let Trish hurt us.

"What on Earth is going on here? Mrs. Warner approaches. Her lips are pinched tight as she narrows her eyes on me. "Ms. Bryant, are you okay?"

Inside my head, I'm screaming for her to help, but I'm too numb to react. I've never felt such hatred before now. I want to hit something or someone. I want to rage out of control, shout at everyone near me, but all I can do is stare at her. There is only one thing clear in my mind. If Trish was anywhere within my reach, nothing would stop me from killing her.

"Please take everyone outside to the playground." Mrs. Warner instructs the teachers. Ms. Giulia calls out for the parents and children to follow her. Hand in hand, Rory, and Carl skip towards the exit door, unaware of the potential danger outside.

"No!" I shove Mrs. Warner to the side in my attempt to reach Rory before she can leave the building. "Rory, stop! You can't go out there."

Lance and Jackson both rush inside, chests heaving, while they visually search the area.

Lance's eyes lock on mine. "Where's Rory?" he shouts.

My hands shake as I point to where Rory is standing beside Mrs. Warner. Jackson walks toward them and kneels to say something too quiet for me to hear. She nods and accepts Jackson's offered hand. He leads her outside with the other children before I can stop them.

"No, wait. Trish is out there." I step forward, but Lance grabs my arm.

"She's safe with Jackson. He won't let anything happen to her."

"But–" he interrupts me.

"You need to tell me what's going on."

"A woman convinced the new teacher she was Rory's Auntie and had her put a gift bag in Rory's cubby." I pick up the pictures from the floor and thrust them at him.

He takes them then speaks calmly into the mic on his shoulder. "10-97 dispatch. Deputy Locke and Deputy Malloy on scene. Code 4, no further assistance is needed."

"Lance, it's Trish. She's the woman who took Rory from the park."

"I know." He keeps his head down, studying the pictures carefully.

"Excuse me?" There's no way I heard him correctly. "You already knew it was Trish?"

"Kellie, let me explain." He holds his hands up defensively.

"Answer me!" I snarl then continue talking through gritted teeth. "Did. You. Know. It. Was. Trish?"

"Yes." He hangs his head, avoiding eye contact.

"That bitch took Rory, and you hid it from me." His betrayal hits me hard and I'm not sure I'll ever be able to forgive him.

12

LANCE

Sweat beads on my brow as I stare at the woman I love. I knew keeping this secret from Kellie would crush her. I've backed myself so far into a corner that I fear she may never forgive me.

"Kellie, please listen." Needing the connection, I reach out to take her hand.

"Don't touch me." She snaps and pulls away.

"You need to understand. My hands were tied. I always suspected Trish but couldn't prove it."

"That doesn't excuse you not telling me."

"I didn't want to worry you."

"It wasn't your call to make, Lance."

"Dispatch to Deputy Locke." The radio call is for Jackson, so I turn the volume down to finish talking with Kellie.

"I'm sorry, Kellie. I thought I was doing the right thing to protect you and Rory."

"And just how does keeping me in the dark do that? What if Trish came to the house while you were at work?"

"She wouldn't dare. We had a plan with a schedule, so you were never alone."

Her jaw drops. "What do you mean, we? Who else knew it was Trish?"

I've said too much, and although I don't have time for this back and forth, continuing to lie won't help. "I told our parents. Even when you took Rory to school, someone was there to protect you in case Trish showed herself."

"Un-fucking-believable. So, you trusted everyone but me." She throws her hands up in the air.

"It wasn't like that." I reach out for her once more but stop myself when she shakes her head. Tears cascade down her cheeks. I've hurt her deeply.

The back door opens, and Jackson walks in, holding Rory's hand.

"There's more." Kellie wipes her face, puts on a smile, and turns to face them. "Hey, kiddo. Can you show Lance your bunny?"

"Catch!" Rory runs over and tosses the stuffed animal to me. "It's my birthday present."

"It was in the bag from Trish," Kellie says in a hushed voice, then lifts Rory into her arms. Her tone no longer holds the anger it did earlier. "I can't believe she was this close to us the whole time." Watching her body tremble, I sense fear and hurt has Kellie in its grips.

"I should have put the pieces together sooner." I'm furious with myself. How could I not figure out that the first bunny came from Trish?

After getting away with taking Rory, Trish must believe she's invincible. However, she made many mistakes today. I'm hoping the school's security cameras recorded her talking with the teacher. That video, along with the other evidence we've gathered, should be enough to prove her guilt beyond a reasonable doubt.

"Lance, turn your radio on. Dispatch said we need to get back to the station."

"What's going on?"

"I sent Javier to the rehab facility to question Trish."

"And?" My knuckles crack as I squeeze the neck of the stuffed rabbit.

"I'm waiting for an update, but I know Sarge wants us back before they bring her in."

"Okay, I just need a moment with Kellie, then I'll meet you outside."

With a raised eyebrow, he looks between Kellie and me. "Alright. Two minutes."

"Lance, I want my bunny." Rory reaches out for her toy.

Reluctantly, I give it back. To her, it's just a gift to celebrate her special day. I'll need to turn it in with the rest of the evidence later, but for now, I don't see the harm in letting her keep it.

I want to stay and plead my case with Kellie but getting Trish into custody takes precedence.

"I have to go. I'll request a car to follow you to your parent's house. Promise me you'll wait for an escort. I need to know you're safe while I'm gone so I can think straight."

Kellie nods. I'm not sure if she can't or won't talk to me. Both hurt equally, but I suppose I deserve it.

"Let me down." Rory squirms and Kellie lowers her to the floor. She quickly latches onto Kellie's legs, holding on tight. It reminds me of the day at the diner. Memories from that day, along with every other since meeting them, are permanently etched in my heart. No matter how hard Trish has tried to separate Kellie and me, she will never be able to take that away.

I try to leave, but the pull to stay close to my family is too strong, keeping my feet from moving. Instead of walking away to do my job, I take this opportunity to express how much I love them.

"I'm sorry for everything." Taking Kellie's hands in mine, I look into her eyes. My heart hurts when I look into her sad eyes that are swollen and red from crying. I remove the monogrammed handkerchief from my pocket. "It wasn't supposed to be like this." Placing it in her hand, I curl her fingers around the carefully folded cloth. "I only wanted to keep you safe. I love you."

I release Kellie's hand and walk outside with the hope that someday, she'll find a way to forgive me.

$\sim$

"Lance, hurry up. We gotta go now." Jackson shouts at me while standing beside his open driver-side door.

"Sorry, I forgot to turn up my radio." I slide into the passenger seat, my mood still shit after leaving Kellie alone to deal with everything she just learned about my deception. "What did I miss?"

"You're not gonna like it." He starts the car and tears out of the parking lot.

"Just tell me."

"They can't find Trish." He turns on the lights and sirens and heads south on Yardley Rd.

"What the hell does that mean?" The hairs on the back of my neck stand on end as adrenaline courses through me.

"Sergeant Williams was able to get information from the guy at the front desk of the hospital. He said Trish checked herself out two nights ago."

"So, where do we go from here?" I try to think of anyone who she might get to help her. From what I last heard, pretty much all of Trish's friends have disowned her.

"First, let's check her dad's house." Jackson slows to go through an intersection then picks up speed again.

"Got it." I pick up the mic from the dash and call dispatch.

"Deputy Malloy and Locke en route to 808 Hillcrest St. ETA five minutes."

"Deputy Mitchell is going to the school to escort Kellie home," Jackson says before I ask.

"Thanks for taking care of that for me."

"Of course." Jackson turns off the lights and sirens when we enter the residential area.

"It's right there. That blue one." I point to the corner house with a new black BMW on the driveway.

He parks on the street. We both exit the vehicle and walk towards the front door.

"I'll take the lead on this," Jackson says. "And make sure your body cam is on."

"Yeah, it's on." I don't wait for him to knock and take some of my frustration out on the door. With the palm of my hand, I pound on the door three times, hard enough to be heard in every corner of the house.

"What is this racket?" Trish's father opens the door. The first thing I notice is how much he's aged since I saw him in court for her voluntary rehab sentencing. His hair is grayer than I remember, and the skin on his face is deeply etched with worry lines. "I've nothing to say to you, Deputy Malloy. Get off my property." He tries to close his door, but Jackson places his boot in the way.

"Sir, my name is Deputy Locke. I need to ask you a few questions about your daughter, Trish. Have you seen her?"

"Patricia is not here."

"He didn't ask that." I snarl, wishing I could knock his pompous ass down a few pegs.

"We have reason to believe your daughter is connected to an incident and need to speak with her." Jackson takes a small notebook from his pocket and flips through the pages. "So, I'll ask again, have you seen her?"

"No, I have not seen my daughter." He keeps his eyes locked on mine while he answers Jackson.

"Perhaps if we tell you that your daughter kidnapped a child, that might jog your memory?" Jackson maintains a high level of professionalism I can't seem to find right now.

"My daughter would never harm a child." His theatrical gasp is almost comical.

I open my mouth to berate this asshole when Jackson takes control of the interview. "I didn't say she did, but she did lure a child away from her family."

"Nonsense. Go talk to her yourself at the rehab facility."

"She's not there," Jackson says bluntly.

"Patricia has to be there. I paid the bill just this morning." It's always about money with him. He didn't even bother to show up in court to support Trish during her hearing. Instead, he sent his high-priced attorney to plead her case.

"Well, maybe if you bothered visiting your daughter, you'd know she checked herself out two nights ago."

"What business is that of yours, Deputy Malloy?" He juts out his chin and looks down his nose at me.

"It became my business when she decided to terrorize my family."

"You can't prove any of that, or you wouldn't be here harassing me."

"I'm warning you. If I find out you've helped Trish evade us, I'll make sure you live to regret it."

"Is that a threat Deputy Malloy?" His gravelly voice doesn't intimidate me one bit.

"Nope. Just doing my job to uphold justice and make sure anyone helping Trish is charged with aiding in the act of a crime, conspiracy, and anything else I can find to put that person away for a very long time."

"How dare you–"

"Don't test me, old man." I step forward and get right in

his face without actually touching him. "No matter how much money you throw around this time, it won't save her. The best thing both of you can do is turn yourselves into the Sheriff's Department and pray the court is lenient."

"Lance." Jackson pulls me back and steps between us.

Red faced, and with steam practically pouring from his ears, he shouts, "Get off my property before I call the Sheriff and report both of you for harassment."

"There's no need to do that." Jackson hands him a business card. "If you hear from her, please contact the Sheriff's Department."

"I'm done with him anyway." I turn to leave while Jackson finishes.

Jackson doesn't take much time to meet me back at the car. Trish's father's attitude only infuriated me. He has always treated his daughter as nothing more than a nuisance. It's too bad he can't be charged with neglect all these years later since his actions are no doubt a significant contributor to Trish's problems as an adult.

"So, what do you think?" I rub the back of my neck, trying to relieve the tension in my muscles. "Should we get a warrant to search the house?"

"No, I don't think she's there, but we can put someone out front just in case."

"That works." I walk to the back of the car and open the trunk. "Do you have any Tylenol in your bag?"

"Yeah." Jackson rifles around in his go-bag then hands me a bottle of water and two pills.

"Thanks." My phone vibrates in my pocket. I just about swallow my tongue when I recognize the number. "No way. Trish is calling."

"You've got to be kidding me?"

I place my finger to my lips to silence him. Tapping my

body camera to activate it for additional evidence, I answer the phone on speaker.

"Hello?"

"Oh, my gosh, Lance. I'm so glad you answered."

"Hello, Trish. Where are you?" I've come on strong and Jackson glares at me.

"I miss you." Her baby talk drove me crazy then and now it's even worse.

Since she ignored my question, I change tactics.

"Aww, baby, I miss you too. Where are you, sweetie?" There's a false perception that police cannot lie while speaking to a suspect. In this circumstance, playing along with her game is entirely legal and admissible in court. Having Jackson as a witness will make the case against Trish even stronger.

"Do you really miss me?" Her voice rises and sounds a bit slurred. I suspect she's either high or drunk off her ass. It should help make it easier to get her talking.

"Yes, honey. I realize what a mistake I made leaving you." My fingernails dig into my palms, and I want to retch for pretending to care about her.

"But I saw you with Kellie last night. You even said you love her."

Jackson has been busy taking notes, but his head snaps up at her admission. We both caught on immediately to what she didn't say. She's been sneaking around outside Kellie's house and was there as recently as last night. He bumps my arms and mouths; *keep going.*

"It was a mistake. Hearing your voice reminds me how much you mean to me. Kellie could never take your place." *You were the mistake.*

"Tell me you still love me," she pleads.

A shiver runs through my body. Everything in me wants to shout that my heart belongs to Kellie and that Trish can rot in hell, but I continue with the charade, knowing it's a means to an end.

"I love you, Patricia." *I hate you! I didn't know what love was until Kellie came into my life.*

"You've made me so happy, Lance. Now I want you to say that you love me more than Kellie and that she means nothing to you."

"Kellie means nothing. I never stopped loving you." *Lies! Kellie is my world.*

"How can I be sure you're not lying to me?"

"Patricia, tell me where you are so I can show you exactly how much I love you."

There's a long pause of silence and I fear the call has dropped.

"Patricia, are you still there?"

"I'm here. Do you remember that cabin by the lake? The one we were stranded at because of the winter storm, and you made love to me all weekend?"

"How could I forget?"

"I'll be there, waiting. I want us to relive that magical moment when you told me you loved me for the first time."

"Perfect. I'm leaving now. Nothing will stop me from getting to you." If she only knew how true that last statement really is.

After calling dispatch to have a deputy sit outside Kellie's parent's house, Jackson and I travel east towards the lake where Trish's dad's fishing cabin sits on several acres of undeveloped private property. It's only ten minutes outside of town. When we get there, I'm surprised to see the large gate leading to the cabin has been left open.

Trish has proven to be unpredictable, and we need to

approach her with the mindset that she is a danger to herself and others. We park at least fifty yards away from the front of the house behind a sizeable grove of trees and bushes to discuss how we plan to enter the home.

"The lights are on and there's smoke coming from the chimney," I whisper. "I don't see her car."

"Maybe it's around back. I'll check the perimeter."

"I'll go to the front door." I reach for the radio on my hip and make some adjustments. We've each put in our earpieces and changed to a private channel so we can communicate.

We exit the car and walk towards the cabin, using the giant redwoods for cover as much as possible.

"Lance, do you copy?" Jackson says quietly into his mic while moving into position.

"10-4. I'm on the move." In case Trish is watching, I casually walk up to the front door and knock. "Patricia, are you in there?" She doesn't respond. Reaching for the doorknob, I turn it, surprised to find it's not locked. I speak softly into my mic. "I'm entering the cabin. I don't have eyes on her yet."

"The back is clear. I'm coming around to you."

Drawing my gun from the holster, I step forward, sweeping the room with my eyes. Trish refers to this as a cabin. However, it's more luxurious than that. There was no way she'd stay in an old log cabin, so she had it renovated from top to bottom. It's about 2000 square feet, single story with an open floorplan kitchen/sitting area, and two bedrooms, each having an attached bathroom.

The only sign that someone has been here recently is the smoldering fire.

"Lance," Jackson says, placing his hand on my back.

"I'll take the master bedroom on the left. You take the other one."

Inching closer towards the open door, I peer around the wall, keeping my body shielded. "Patricia, it's Lance. Where are you, sweetheart?" I step inside when there's still no answer.

My eyes travel immediately to the message spray-painted to the wall above the bed.

"You lied to me."

"Fuck! Jackson, follow me." I shout while running out the front door.

"What's going on?"

"She's going after Kellie." Jackson and I sprint to the car. "Call the unit that's supposed to be at Kellie's parents to check on her."

"On it." Jackson jumps into the driver's seat and barely waits for me to close my door before taking off. With the lights flashing and sirens blaring, he speeds away from the property, turning in the direction of Kellie's parent's house. I look at my watch and figure it will take at least fifteen minutes to get there.

Jackson calls dispatch, and I dial Kellie's phone number. "Come on, pick up, babe." It rings twice and goes to voice-mail. "Kellie. You need to stay at your parent's house. I think Trish is trying to find you. Call me immediately."

"Kellie's not answering my call. What's going on with the patrol you sent over to her parent's house?"

"Deputy Fisher should be there in five minutes."

"Tell him to check in as soon as he gets on scene." I call Kellie one more time with still no answer. "Where the hell is she?"

13

KELLIE

While driving back to my house. Lance's name appears on my car's console touchscreen. Ignoring the call, I press decline and grumble, "I can't deal with you right now." Between the incident at school and discovering that he lied to me, my emotions are all over the place. When it rings again, I switch my phone to silent. He can leave a message if it's important.

I forget Lance for the moment and think of Trish. My blood boils, but knowing she's screwed up and will be arrested is the only good thing that has happened today. Still, I'm not looking forward to dealing with a trial, but if it means keeping my family safe, there's no way I'll back down. However brave I might feel right now, my biggest fear is the negative effects these next few months may have on Rory.

"Damn it." I bang my hand on the steering wheel. "Why couldn't he just trust me?" Tears of frustration and hurt have dried up, leaving a dull ache in my heart. There's no sense in wasting my energy on self-pity. It's time to pull myself together and fix one of the biggest parenting mistakes I've ever made.

Before Deputy Williams left my parent's house, I gave him the stuffed rabbit for evidence. It was that or rip it to shreds, just like Tigress did the first one. There's no way I want anything connected to Trish around us.

Unfortunately, I wasn't thinking straight and didn't realize Rory was watching the hand-off. She's devastated that her birthday present was taken away from her. The only thing I could think to do was drive home to pick up a few of her favorite toys. My heart broke just a little more when she asked me to bring Mr. Deputy Bear. Her request brought me back to my own deputy and how different Lance looked before he left.

While he's in uniform, I've become accustomed to the stoic expression he wears like armor. The firm set of his jaw makes him appear emotionless and unapproachable when in reality, he's quietly observing his surroundings for any potential threats the public may not see. He stands confidently with his shoulders back, chest out, and chin high, silently assuring anyone watching he's there to protect them.

Each day, I watch as he unknowingly turns up the volume on these characteristics before walking out the door then turns them down when the uniform comes off. A little piece of it always stays in place, but not today.

This time Lance lowered his guard completely. He showed me the vulnerability behind the badge. His shoulders were slumped inward, and his chin dipped to his chest. Instead of the icy, hard stare, his eyes were soft and focused only on me. Lance let his walls down just enough for me to hear the sincerity in his words.

"I only wanted to keep you safe."

I know he wouldn't intentionally hurt me and that keeping Trish away from us was his goal. It's how he did it that bothers me. But thinking more about his actions, is it that far-fetched to think Lance was doing the right thing by keeping it a secret? Especially after finding out about the baby. As I continue to dissect what Lance did, a seed of doubt is planted in my mind. Maybe I'm the one that should have trusted his decision and listened instead of shutting him down so quickly.

Out of the blue, a conversation Lance and I had months ago about how his career might affect our relationship comes to mind. I remember how serious he was while ticking off each item. It felt like he was trying to talk me out of dating him by only pointing out the negative side of being with a cop.

I was already dealing with his irregular work schedule and saw first-hand the emotional toll the job takes on the entire family. But the part I'd forgotten about until now was Lance telling me how his hypervigilance works. Both on and off duty, he's assessing the current situation and how to react should danger present itself. And if it does, he promised me that he would do whatever it takes to protect his family. When it comes down to it, keeping those around him safe has become second nature to Lance and is just another reason I love him.

I stop at a red light and try to rationalize what Lance did. "I guess he didn't really lie," I huff out. The light changes to green and I turn down the road that leads to my house.

Parking in the driveway, I exit the car and walk to the front door. Now that I've had time to process all that has happened, I want to talk to him, but it should be face to face and not over the phone. I unlock the screen and consider sending Lance a message when a text comes in from him.

Lance: What's your 20?

Great. He's using his codes again. *Is he asking where I am?* I should remember, but my mind is cluttered with other things.

Kellie: I'm at my house. I'll call you when I'm done.

I don't wait for his reply. Instead, shoving my phone in my back pocket, then dig in my purse for the keys. Entering the house, I hang my key on the hook beside the light switch and kick my shoes off.

Usually, Tigress comes running once the door opens, but she's nowhere to be seen. "Here, kitty kitty." She's probably pouting because I didn't feed her yet. "Tigress," I call and click my tongue. "I don't have time for your attitude, missy." I open the pantry, pour her dry food into the dish, and fill her water bowl. "It's here whenever you get hungry."

I stroll down the hall to my room. As I push the door open, I just about jump out of my skin when Tigress bolts around the corner. My gaze follows her into the kitchen. Placing the palm of my hand against my chest, I feel the rapid thudding of my heart. "Damn cat, you almost gave me a heart attack."

I take a few steps into my bedroom, horrified by what I see. All of my picture frames have been torn from the walls and smashed. The white goose-down comforter and pillows have been slashed. Feathers are scattered everywhere, and broken glass litters the floor. Everything has been destroyed.

"It's not the cat you should be worrying about, Kellie." Spinning around, I meet the evil gaze of the woman determined to ruin my life.

"Trish, what the fuck are you doing in my house?" She walks into my room, shoving me to the side as she passes. I stumble back until my shoulders make contact with the wall.

She looks nothing like she did at her last court appearance. Her dark hair has been bleached blonde and cut to shoulder length. I can only assume she's done this in an attempt to disguise herself.

The rest of her transformation hits too close to home. Trish's once flawless complexion is now marred with the familiar small scars of a drug addict. I recognize the signs of picking at the invisible bugs under her skin often associated with methamphetamine use. She's not entirely covered with the sores yet, but it will only worsen unless she stops using.

If I had to guess, Trish found more substances to abuse while in rehab. Leslie went through the same thing. The safe place where addicts go to recover can sometimes expose the patients to drugs they may never have used before trying to get clean. She's fallen into the same dark place my sister never returned from. It's a sickness and nothing I'd wish on anyone, even Trish. But with the crazed look in her eyes, my only concern is to get out of here alive.

"You can't really be this stupid?"

My gaze is fixed on the knife as she slides the sharp edge back and forth against her thigh. She doesn't flinch when the blade cuts through the material of her white yoga pants, piercing her skin. "I don't understand what you want from me." A trickle of blood seeps from the wound into the material. The smell of copper and the crimson stain causes me to gag.

"Why do you think I'm here, Saint Kellie?"

"Trish, stop. Look what you're doing to your leg." She glances down and shakes her head like the blood dripping onto the floor means nothing. "If you let me go, I won't say anything to Lance or the police."

"Shut up, bitch!" She raises the knife high and plunges it into the mattress with a maniacal laugh.

For the first time in my life, I'm worried about ever seeing my family again.

"Trish, I'll do whatever you want." I slide my back along the wall while sidestepping away from her towards the hall.

"You know Lance doesn't love you, right? In fact, I have a message from him that I think you'll really enjoy." She removes her phone from her pocket then turns it so I can see the screen. It's an image of Lance with a huge smile. However, it doesn't appear to be a current picture. His hair is longer, and he looks much younger.

She presses play and Lance's deep voice comes through the speaker clear as day. "Kellie means nothing." It stops and she swipes down to the next message. "I never stopped loving you, Patricia."

My stomach flips. Hearing Lance say I meant nothing to him knocks the air from my lungs.

With a smug expression settling on her lips, she edges closer and plays it again. As much as I don't want to hear Lance's cruel words, I listen carefully. That's when I pick up on the subtle change in Lance's tone. He's lying to her. I recognize the detached and impersonal voice he uses while on the job. It's not the same as the one he uses when telling me he loves me.

"So, as you can hear, Lance doesn't love you and never did." She throws her head back and cackles, playing the part of an evil villain to perfection.

Trish is insane and so emotionally committed to her version of the truth I'll never be able to change her mind. My best chance of getting away from her is to go along with what she's saying.

"You're right. I give up." Dipping my chin to my chest to show defeat, I intend to give the performance of my life. "I always knew he loved you and he was using me. I won't stand in your way. Lance is all yours."

She rolls her eyes dramatically and plucks the knife from the mattress. "You think it's that easy. You give up and I'll simply walk away like nothing ever happened." She grabs my arm and pulls me towards the bathroom. I try to struggle against her hold until she places the blade against my belly. "You ruined my plans when you trapped him with this baby. Now I need to figure out how to get rid of you for good."

"Wait, Trish, don't do this." I splay my free hand over my stomach, nicking my finger on the knife. "Please don't hurt my baby. I promise I'll tell Lance I don't want him around."

"You're nothing but a badge bunny whore." Trish drags me out of the room towards the bathroom. "I have one more thing I need to do before I'm ready to end this once and for all."

Tigress darts in front of us, taking Trish's attention away from me for the briefest of seconds. It gives me the opening I need to fight back. I pull away from her grasp, step forward, and shove the heel of my palm into her face. The knife falls from her hand, landing with a loud clang on the hardwood floor.

"Fuck," Trish cries out, wiping away the blood running down her lips.

Falling to my knees, I grab the knife before she reaches for it.

"Give me the knife," she growls from between gritted teeth.

I'm not stupid. Trish has no intention of letting me live. Years ago, my father told Leslie and me never to give up if we were ever attacked. Get up and keep fighting until you can get away safely. If you stay down, they will have all the power.

Trish stands over me, rears back, and kicks me in the ribs.

I turn away to protect my belly before she lands the next kick. An instinct to survive overrules the pain in my side. I scramble to stand, using the wall for support. "Fuck you." I lunge forward, slamming my shoulder into her stomach. I drive forward until her back hits the wall.

"I hate you," she screams and pounds her fist against my back. "He's mine."

"You've lost your mind." I drop the knife and use both hands to push Trish onto the ground. She still has a fistful of my hair and takes me down with her. I land another punch to her face. She lets go of me, giving me the chance to stand and race to the back door.

With shaky hands coated with Trish's blood, I struggle to turn the knob. Looking back over my shoulder, I see she's still on the floor, clutching her face and moaning in pain.

Wiping my hands on my pants, I'm finally able to grip the knob and pull the door open. I run outside and check my pockets for my keys. *Shit, they're hanging on the hook beside the front door.*

Trish's blood-curdling screams can be heard from inside the house. Suddenly she appears and stumbles down the back steps. The sun reflects off something in her hand.

Shit, where did she get a gun? I slide back under the thick bushes that sit behind the garden bench.

Frantically, I turn in a circle looking for a place to hide. Ducking down, I pull out my phone to call for help. My lock screen is full of missed messages from Lance he sent while my phone was on silent.

Lance: We can't find Trish.

Lance: Answer your phone.

Lance: Where the fuck are you?

I quit scrolling the notifications and unlock the phone. I

don't have time to type everything, so I use the codes Lance drilled into me.

Kellie: Home. Help.

Kellie: 10-35.

Please be the right one to call for backup.

Lance: I'm coming. Are you safe?

Kellie: No.

Lance: Is Trish there?

Kellie: Yes.

Sweat drips from my brow, burning my eyes. She's only a few feet in front of me. I hold my breath, trying to stay as still as possible. When she turns around, I look at my screen.

Lance: 10-35

Lance: ETA five minutes.

"Thank God," I whisper. Taking a deep breath, I groan. The pain from where Trish kicked me feels like a white-hot steel rod has been jammed into my side.

"So, there you are." Trish looks in my direction. "You thought you could hide from me?" She creeps closer, squats down, and points the gun at me. Blood is smeared across her face, but it doesn't hide the bruises forming on her cheeks.

"Please, Trish. Don't do this. Think about your family."

My voice cracks. I need to stall her, so Lance has time to find me.

"Ha. They never gave a shit about me. I heard their whispers. Saw the way they looked at me, with pity, like I was crazy and that I didn't matter. Her eyes shine with tears, and for a moment, I think I've gotten through to her. "Do you know, my own father once told me he wished I'd never been born."

"I'm sorry, Trish, but if you let me, I can help you."

Her expression changed in an instant to one of curiosity. "You mean like you helped your sister?" Then she chuckled. "Poor Leslie died a fucked-up junkie and you stepped right in and stole her baby."

I want to tear her hair out but had to remain calm. "You're right. I failed Leslie, but I won't fail you if you just give me a chance."

"Get up. I'm tired of hearing your good girl preaching. You don't know what I've gone through." I crawl out from under the bush and wince when I stand. I'm not feeling good and the pain in my side is worsening, but I can't give up now.

"Where are we going?"

"Somewhere, you'll never see Lance or your bratty niece ever again." She pushes me forward. "Now, move."

Dad's words come back to me again. *Don't let them take you anywhere. Run, fight back, get somewhere safe.* With every ounce of strength I can muster, I elbow her in the face and race off to the front of the house, praying someone is there to help.

14

LANCE

"I swear to God, Jackson, if Trish hurts her, I'll fucking–"

"Don't go there," he interrupts while focusing on the road. "Kellie's smart and she knows we're on our way."

"You better be right. Come on, step on it."

He does as I ask and increases his speed. Not wanting to alert Trish to our arrival, I shut off the lights and sirens. We're only a few houses away from Kellie's when the loud crack of a single gunshot echoes across the neighborhood.

"Shit!" Jackson slams on his brakes and grabs the mic from the dash. "Dispatch, shots fired. 10-35 request backup."

Before Jackson can put the car in park, I fling open the door and use it for cover while scanning the area. My training overrides my desire to run in with guns blazing, but I know we don't have time to wait for other officers to arrive either.

"Hurry up. It sounded like it came from behind Kellie's house." We cautiously approach, doing our best to stay covered behind cars and trees.

Just as we round the corner to her property, Kellie darts

from the opposite side of the house, and runs across the street. Trish is only steps behind her.

Holstering my weapon, adrenaline pumps through me as I run after them. Pain from the ankle I injured while looking for Rory shoots up my leg with each pounding step I take. I don't have to look back to know Jackson's location. The rattling of the keys on his duty belt and heavy boots hitting the pavement tells me he's got my back.

"Sheriff's Department, stop running and show me your hands," Jackson calls out.

Kellie glances over her shoulder, her eyes wide with fear. "Lance, she has a gun."

"Stay where you are or I'll shoot her," Trish shouts while gaining ground on Kellie.

Suddenly Kellie turns and crosses the road as Trish reaches out to grab her and misses, screeching her frustration.

"I'm gonna kill you and that thing growing inside you."

"Stay away from me." Kellie's steps look heavy as she slows. She's getting tired, but I still can't seem to get to her fast enough.

"It'll be quick," she teases. "Just close your eyes and think of Leslie and Paul both burning in hell–you'll be with them soon enough."

Kellie stumbles in the middle of the road and Trish reaches her before I can.

"Let her go," I snarl, desperate to get to her.

"Aw, isn't that sweet? Your knight in shining armor is here to rescue you."

"Because he loves me, you twisted bitch."

"Get up." Trish glares and reaches down, yanking Kellie to her feet by the arm.

I lunge forward, ready to fight, but Jackson grabs me by the shoulder, pulling me to the side of a large truck. I know what the proper procedures are, but right now, all reason has left me.

"You're going to get us all killed." He shoves me hard against the bed of the truck, knocking the wind from my lungs. "Use your fucking head or your girl will die."

"Let me go," I growl, grasping at Jackson's wrists while fighting to get him off me.

"We don't have time for this asshole," Jackson shoves me once more.

Knowing he's right, I stop battling him. "Do it, Jackson!" I draw my gun but keep it pointed down. "Get her away from Kellie or I will."

"Cover me." Jackson stays low and peers around the truck's fender. "This doesn't look good, Lance."

I look over his shoulder to see what he's talking about. Trish is a mess with dried blood smeared across her face and her shirt is torn at the collar. She's using Kellie as a human shield and holds the gun down by her side. Kellie's breathing is labored, and her eyes are red from crying, but overall, she seems unharmed. The blood on her shirt appears to be from Trish. Between the two of them, Trish is definitely worse off physically.

"Show me your hands now," Jackson takes aim at Trish and makes his demands while I use my radio to give an update.

"Dispatch, Deputy Locke has one at gunpoint. Suspect has one known female hostage. Keep this channel clear." Standing back and just waiting for Trish to pull the trigger doesn't sit right with me, but I trust Jackson for now.

"Patricia," Jackson says calmly. "I just want to talk to you."

"Let me talk to Lance or I'll blow her head off." Trish roars back.

Fuck this shit. If it's me she wants, then that's what I'll give her. I holster my gun and step into the open. This isn't part of my training, but Trish is on a short fuse. This situation needs to be de-escalated immediately if we are going to get out of it without anyone getting hurt.

"Lance, damn it!" Jackson tries pulling me back, but I shrug him off.

"I won't let her use Kellie as a bargaining chip." Talking to Jackson in a hushed tone, I remain forward facing to keep my gaze on Trish and Kellie.

"Fine but stay back and keep her talking. I'll try to find a better position." With me between him and Trish, there's no way he'd ever be able to get off a good shot without moving to a new spot.

"I'm right here." I stand with my arms out wide, completely exposed. "Come on, babe, let her go. Then we can be together, just like you want." I need Trish to believe she is my world and that all I want is her. I watch Kellie's expression closely. When she dips her chin slightly, I know she understands what I'm trying to do.

"Please just let me go," Kellie pleads with Trish.

She laughs. "Shut up."

"Trish, sweetheart, focus on me," I say, worried how the next few moments will play out. She doesn't look at me.

"Once you're dead, Lance will love me again, just like he used to before you stole him from me." She raises the gun.

Anxiety takes a tight hold of me. "I'm begging you, don't do this. Think about how this will affect the rest of your life."

"You don't get it, Lance. Without you, I have no life." She looks at me and with a strange expression, takes aim, and fires the gun in my direction. The bullet narrowly misses me as I dive to the ground.

"No!" Kellie roars.

"Lance, I don't have a clear shot," Jackson calls over the radio.

"Kellie, run…" I shout, terrified Trish will shoot her next.

Before I can get to my feet, Kellie swings her elbow wildly, knocking Trish onto the asphalt, allowing her the opportunity to run.

Trish doesn't stay down and gives chase. She's right behind Kellie, screaming like a banshee. "I'm gonna catch you, and when I do, you're dead."

I make my move, and despite the pain in my ankle, I push through it. Jackson is already in pursuit and is just a few yards behind them with me bringing up the rear. Cars continue to drive down the street, oblivious to the danger that surrounds them.

Kellie turns to cross the street, slipping between two parked cars with Trish gaining ground.

Suddenly, a horn blares as the speeding SUV barely misses Kellie but slams directly into Trish. The impact sends her flying backward.

I watch in horror as her head smashes against the pavement in a sickening crunch.

Kellie stops and turns to look at the carnage behind her.

I can tell she's going to try and help. "No," I call out, getting closer, but it doesn't appear she's listening.

I reach Trish at the same time Kellie does. She's in shock and doesn't seem to register my presence.

"Kellie, are you hurt?" She doesn't respond.

I look over my shoulder to see Jackson speaking to the elderly male driver who hit Trish. He's understandably shaken. Jackson catches my gaze and I slowly shake my head. He picks up on my message and escorts the man over to the sidewalk to sit. Trish's selfish behavior has left a scar on this stranger's life that will never fully heal.

Kellie kneels at Trish's side and takes her hand, showing compassion I know I'm not capable of. "Trish, can you hear me?"

Trish turns her head slightly, a trickle of blood running from her mouth.

"Hold on, please," Kellie begs, her eyes streaming with tears.

"Lance never loved you." Trish's gaze settles on Kellie.

"Help is on the way," I say for Kellie's sake, as I feel nothing but contempt for Trish.

Kellie holds Trish's hand, trying her best to offer comfort I'm certain isn't wanted. "Come on, stay with me. It won't be long now."

I can hear the desperation in Kellie's tone, but I know it's too late to do anything.

Trish coughs, and a stream of blood runs down her cheek.

"Lance, do something, please," Kellie begs me, wide-eyed.

Seeing as many accidents as I have, I know I'm powerless to help. "It's best not to move her."

"Lance, please..." Her words trail off because, deep down, she knows there is too much damage.

Trish's head lolls to the side. A single tear falls as she takes her last breath.

Then, for a few seconds, there is absolute silence.

"Kellie, she's gone." Contempt is replaced with feelings of regret and mourning a wasted life.

"No, no, no," Kellie cries, slumping forward as I drop to the ground and pull her into my arms.

15

KELLIE

I stare out of the second-story window, watching as men and women in dress uniforms gather in small clusters, engaged in conversation. Occasionally someone new will approach a group, and handshakes will be exchanged along with a few pats on the back. I recognize a few faces, but mainly the crowd is full of people I've never met. They are Lance's friends and fellow officers who have come to support one of their brothers in blue.

Today is a special day that almost never was.

Seven months ago, Trish turned my world upside down. Her actions had far-reaching consequences that are still being felt by many. Gina and her family were beside themselves and full of remorse, though the responsibility was not theirs to take. Shortly after Trish died, her dad quit his job, sold their house, and disappeared. He didn't even have the good grace to bury his only daughter before leaving town. It was probably for the best, as it gave those who cared about Trish a sense of closure.

It was Gina's parents who handled the funeral arrangements and held a private burial for their niece. Lance and I attended but came in after the service had already started. We sat quietly in the far corner of the church, allowing Trish's family to mourn without my presence upsetting them.

I needed my own closure, and although Lance didn't understand why it was important to me, he didn't complain. Instead, he sat by my side and comforted me by wiping away my tears. Seeing Trish die the way she did is something I'll never fully get over.

The truth is, I can't bring myself to hate Trish because I know there had to be a time when she was a good person or Lance would never have been attracted to her. Sadly, she was already lost by the time our paths crossed. Drugs and alcohol became her crutch, leading her down a dark road she couldn't escape. Just as Leslie had done. So even though Trish would have killed me had things gone her way, it's not in me to live with hate for a person who will never have the opportunity to make amends for her actions.

"Kel, is everything alright," Gina asks, and I turn to face her. She's absolutely gorgeous in her navy-blue sheath dress. Even if she does look a little like a penguin trying to sneak a beach ball into a movie theater. In three months, she and Dirk will be welcoming little Angelica into the world.

"Yeah, I'm okay." I draw in a deep breath. "I promised myself I wouldn't cry, and yet here I am reflecting and letting my emotions take over."

"Trish again?" Gina knows me too well. "You're such a good person, Kellie. Nobody else would forgive and move on the way you have."

"Holding on to anger is part of what destroyed Trish. Dwelling on the past is a waste of my time. There are far too many beautiful things in my life to allow any of that to over-shadow my future."

"I love you, Kel," she sniffles and leans in to hug me but is blocked by her baby bump.

"I love you too." I blow her a kiss, and she pretends to catch it.

"What did I miss?" Melanie ambles up with three champagne flutes. "Two famous mimosas and one sparkling cider for the chubby one who's gonna waddle down the aisle."

"Hey, that was supposed to be me." I smack her arm playfully.

"Well, look on the bright side," Melanie says. "Your dress looks banging on those tiny hips."

I run my hands over my flat belly. Looking at my reflection in the full-length mirror, I have to agree with her. I look and feel much better than I ever thought I would. After being kicked and thrown around by Trish, my recovery was slow, and I suffered several complications. Eventually, I made it through to the other side.

"Let me see your ring again, and when you tell the story about how Lance gave it to you, don't leave anything out." Underneath Melanie's tough exterior lives a sappy romantic.

"Last time," I giggle and take a sip of my mimosa. "When we got to the hospital after the, you know, the terrible incident with your cousin, Lance asked where I'd put the handkerchief he'd given me earlier that day."

"Yeah, go on. This is my favorite part." Melanie claps excitedly.

"You're hopeless." I finish the cocktail and place it on the side table. "Okay, as I was saying. Lance asked, and I told him it was in my pocket. I was lying down, black and blue, from getting my ass kicked, and couldn't reach it, so he dug it out of my pocket and handed it to me. It was still folded up. When he told me to open it, a diamond ring fell out and onto my belly."

"And that's when he said it wasn't supposed to be like this.

The same words he used when he gave it to you at the school." Gina shrieks.

"Then he professed his undying love for you, right there in the hospital, and all the staff started cheering when he slid the ring on your finger." Melanie sighs.

"Why do you make me repeat this story if y'all know it by heart?" Secretly I love retelling it because it helps to drown out the parts from the day I'd rather forget.

"Because it belongs in the hall of fame for proposals. Lancelot is an amazing man, but he's lucky to have you in his life."

"Aww, you girls are really trying to ruin my makeup, aren't you?" We group hug and squeal like schoolgirls. Rory comes and tugs on my hand wanting to get in on the love fest.

"Addy K. Do you like my dress?" She twirls around in her white dress that was handmade to match mine. Rory's has several extra layers of ruffles and a navy sash that matches Gina and Melanie's dresses.

"You are perfect, baby."

"I'm not a baby." She crosses her arms over her chest and pooches out her bottom lip.

"I'm sorry, you're right. You're a big girl."

"It's okay, Addy K, I still love you." With a smile that melts my heart, she rushes off across the room to talk with Lance's mom.

"She sure says the darndest things?" Gina laughs.

"That she does," I agree.

"Just wait, your little one is going to pick up all of Rory's bad habits, too," Melanie adds while rubbing Gina's tummy.

"You all look beautiful." Mom kisses my cheek and holds my gaze in the reflection of the full-length mirror. She's been through hell and back between Leslie's death, Rory's kidnapping, and my accident, but you wouldn't know it. In my mom, I see a lioness. Strong, proud, and fierce. I can only dream of being the pillar of strength that my mom is.

With a knot the size of a grapefruit filling my throat, I'm only able to mouth; I love you.

Dad clears his throat when entering the room. "It's time, ladies."

Everyone scrambles to gather their flowers and take one final look before walking down the stairs to line up.

"Kellie, where's your bouquet?" the wedding coordinator asks, searching through empty boxes.

"I don't have one," I reach out and take my newborn baby girl, Leslie Grace, from my father's arms, then hold out my hand for Rory. She squeezes my hand and grins up at me. This day is just as special for her. She's gaining a father she can always depend on to protect her and I'm marrying the man of my dreams. Life couldn't be any better than it is right now.

16

LANCE

"It's now or never." Jackson claps my shoulder. "I've got the squad car all set if you want to escape."

"There's no chance of that happening. I've wanted this from the first time I saw Kellie. I only wish it could have been sooner." I look around the large crowd of officers, family, and friends. There must be at least a hundred people milling about.

Kellie and I planned for this to be a small ceremony, but once everyone found out we were getting married, the guest list grew to the point we both threw up our hands and said the more, the merrier. So now the house is surrounded by squad cars, and the garden is filled with cops from all over the county.

My only request was for Kellie to have the wedding of her dreams.

Gina's parents graciously offered their home for the celebration, and the sun is just beginning to set. Exactly the way Kellie had hoped. We had to make a few adjustments and push the date back when Kellie went into labor three and a half weeks early, but everything has worked out for the best. We're here now and I can't wait to make her my wife.

"Alright Loverboy, that smile on your face is all I needed to see."

"Thanks, Jackson. Not just for standing beside me today, but for everything else you've done to help me this year. I wouldn't be here without your support."

"Yeah, you would have. You're a great man, Lance. The obstacles that you and Kellie faced couldn't stop the love and devotion you have for one other." Jackson is more than my partner. He's the older brother I never had, who I look up to and respect personally and professionally. "You deserve to be happy."

"Thanks, now hand over your godson so we can get this show on the road."

I hold out my hands and carefully lift my baby boy out of Jackson's arms. Phillip Paul and his twin sister, Leslie Grace, are only a month old.

After being brutally assaulted by Trish, Kellie suffered cramping and bleeding. It scared the life out of me and on doctor's order, she grumbled through an entire month of bed rest. During that time, I wouldn't let her lift a finger which drove her crazy, but I'd do anything to keep my family safe, and she knows that.

It was during that time we discovered she was carrying twins. Wanting some sort of normality and much needed peace and quiet, we chose to keep it a secret until we knew for sure both babies were healthy. Once we received the all-clear, asking Jackson to be godfather to our twins was a no-brainer. No matter what he says, I know that without him my life would look very different right now.

"Gentlemen, please take your places so we may begin." The wedding coordinator directs Jackson and me to stand at the end of the aisle in front of the gazebo.

"Last chance," Jackson says while trying not to move his lips.

"Shut up," I chuckle. "Just wait until you find the one who makes life worth living. Then it's my turn to harass you."

Phillip squirms in my arms until I move him into a position that settles him. He closes his eyes and drifts back to sleep, unaware of what's about to happen.

Time seems to slow as I take in the enormity of this moment. The gentle notes of Kellie's chosen song, Love Never Fails by Brandon Heath, begin as the bridesmaids walk towards us. I lean over to look down the aisle and see Kellie. She's holding our daughter, Leslie Grace, close to her heart and Rory is right by her side, clutching the lace of her white gown.

The sun glints off the gold heart locket we gave Rory last night to commemorate this special day. The papers have already been submitted for Kellie and me to adopt her. It's just a formality because I already feel that Rory is my daughter, even without the court making it official.

I think most men would be freaking out with newborn twins and a four-year-old, but not me because today isn't just about Kellie and I becoming man and wife. It's also a celebration of our family and how fortunate we are to have three happy and healthy children.

Kellie's father places her left hand in mine.

"Look after my little girl, Lance."

"Yes, sir."

Kellie passes our daughter over to Melanie while Jackson takes Phillip from me.

"Do you want to stand beside me or go sit with Gram Gram?" Kellie whispers to Rory. Even though our ceremony is short, we decided to give her a choice.

"Over there," she says, then skips over to sit beside Kellie's mom.

I take Kellie's hands in mine and turn to face Chaplain Tillmon.

"Welcome, friends and family. We are gathered here today to witness and celebrate the union of Lance Malloy and Kellie Bryant in marriage. We offer our love and support, so they may begin married life surrounded by those dearest to them."

While the chaplain continues, I allow my thoughts to wander, not really taking in his words. Instead, I stare at Kellie, dazzled by all that she is, and thank God fate brought her to me. She is the one I want standing beside me for the rest of my life and the only one I trust to help me carry the weight of the badge.

"Both Lancelot and Kellie have written their own vows. Lance, would you like to start."

I'm suddenly brought back to the moment with a nudge from Kellie.

"Yes, sorry," I mumble as the guests chuckle.

"Take your time," the chaplain says.

"Kellie, I never believed in love at first sight until I met you. From that moment on, my heart and soul knew you were the one I would spend the rest of my life with. It just took us some time to get here. I adore you and promise to spend every day of my life showing you just how much I love you." There was so much more I planned to say, but looking into Kellie's eyes, I knew it wasn't necessary.

"Do you, Lancelot, take this woman to be your wife?" Chaplain Tillmon asks me the biggest question of my life.

"I do."

"And now, Kellie..." he says while turning to her.

"Lancelot, you are the man I've always dreamed of finding but didn't believe existed. You are my one true love, best friend, and soul mate. I promise to stand by your side and support you through the good times and bad. Today, before our family and friends, I promise to spend the rest of my life loving you." Kellie's eyes shine bright. Even with tears streaming down her face, she's smiling from ear to ear.

"Do you, Kellie, take this man to be your husband?"

"I do."

I remove the new monogrammed handkerchief from my pocket to gently wipe away her tears. Mom had it made especially for today. It's hand-embroidered with the initials of our first names and the date. I tuck it back into my pocket, ready for the next wave of emotions to take over both of us.

"Lance and Kellie have chosen to exchange rings as a symbol of their unending love. As you place the ring on Kellie's finger, please repeat after me."

"I got this," I say to more chuckles from watching friends and family. I'm not nervous because I've spent weeks trying to memorize the next part. So rather than wait, I jump right into it. "With this ring, I, Lancelot Thomas Malloy, take thee, Kellie Ann Bryant, to be my wedded wife, to have and to hold from this day forward, for better for worse, in sickness and in health, to love and to cherish, till death us do part."

I breathe a sigh of relief as I slip the ring onto Kellie's finger though I'm not done yet.

"I give you this ring as a symbol of my love with the pledge: to love you today, tomorrow, always, and forever."

It's the chaplain's turn to speak once more. "Now, to you, Kellie."

"I think I got this too," Kellie says, drawing a bigger smile from me. "Sorry…" She wears a sheepish grin.

"That's quite alright." The chaplain says good-naturedly. "Whenever you're ready."

"I, Kellie Ann Bryant, take thee, Lancelot Thomas Malloy, to be my wedded husband, to have and to hold from this day forward, for better for worse, in sickness and in health, to love and to cherish, till death us do part."

She slips the ring onto my finger. "I give you this ring as a symbol of my love with the pledge: to love you today, tomorrow, always, and forever."

We're almost there, I tell myself.

"By the power vested in me, I pronounce you husband and wife. You may kiss your bride."

It was a simple kiss, just like the first one we shared only this time, when our lips met, it spoke of true love, commitment, and the promises we'd just made to one another.

"It is with the greatest of pleasure to officially introduce Deputy Lancelot & Mrs. Kellie Malloy."

We turn to face our family and friends to a roar of congratulations. Kellie reaches out for Leslie. Melanie settles her in Kellie's arms while I reach for Phillip. Rory cheers along with the others then rushes over to stand with us. As moments go, I couldn't ask for anything more perfect than this.

"Are you ready?" I ask, giving Kellie's hand a squeeze.

"Yep, I think so." Her eyes glisten with unshed tears. There's one final part to our ceremony that's important to us. For a moment, the sounds of people celebrating fade away. The sun has almost set and the tiny lights around the gazebo twinkle in the fading daylight, bathing us and our surroundings in a heavenly glow.

With my wife's hand in mine, our babies snuggled close, and Rory clinging to Kellie's dress, we pause and look at the two empty chairs in the front row, flanking either side of the aisle. We intentionally left them vacant in honor of two family members who could not be with us on this important day.

One represents Leslie, who should have been standing by Kellie's side today as her maid of honor.

The other represents my best man, Paul.

"I miss her so much." Kellie looks up into my eyes and I see the pain and guilt she's carrying still.

"I know, I miss Paul too."

"Do you think they were watching us today?"

"Yeah, I really do."

I let go of her hand and wrap my arm around her shoulders, pulling her into me. I couldn't ask for a more loving bride or a better family. All eyes are on us, but I don't care. I won't rush her. This is more than just remembering the ones we love whose lives were tragically cut short. They will forever be a piece of our lives and the reason we are a family today. But it's time to start living without regrets or feeling haunted by our pasts.

I lean in and kiss her, wanting to push away the sadness that has crept in.

"I think it's time." Kellie looks up to me, her eyes shining brighter than the sun.

"I agree." I look over to Rory who's been amazingly patient today. "Are you ready, little miss?"

"Yep." She nods and leaves Kellie's side to stand beside me. I switch Philip over to lay his head on the opposite shoulder and take Rory's hand. "Lance, is it time for cake now?"

Kellie and I chuckle. "Yeah, it's cake time."

She can't hide her excitement and tugs on my hand. "I want lots and lots…"

"Come on then. Let's go," I say.

As we make our way down the aisle to celebrate with our friends and family, the joy and laughter from all around us fill our hearts.

"After everything we've been through, I can't believe I'm finally Mrs. Malloy."

"Never in my wildest dreams did I believe I'd find somebody like you."

"I feel like I'm living in a dream."

"You are baby. But I'm right there with you."

"I love you, Sir Lancelot."

I look into her eyes and am reminded how blessed I truly am. "I love you too, wife."

THE END

A NOTE FROM KAYLEE

A note from Kaylee:

Thank you for reading The Weight of the Badge. Writing this series took me over two years from start to finish. It has been a labor of love full of tears, heartache, and angst, mixed with laughter, smiles, and the happily ever after I always wanted. It just took longer to get there than I initially planned.

Lance and Kellie's story was plotted as a single book. Everything was to be sewn up in a neat HEA package. But the struggles and pain this couple went through were far too big to gloss over. With guidance from my editor, this story grew into what you see today.

The Weight of the Badge has always been more than a romance novel for me. It is written to honor the first responder community and spread awareness of the rising numbers of suicides and mental health issues they and their families face. I can only hope that one day speaking up and asking for help won't be so hard for those who need it.

Thank you again for taking this journey with me.

Coming Soon from

Kaylee Rose and Zane Michaelson

ROMAN: Hot In the City - The Whole Story

For Roman, sexual gratification is the ultimate high; addictive and all-consuming. It must be attained, no matter the cost to himself or the Blackthorne family reputation.

Considered by many to be handsome, arrogant, and tough, within him sits a ruthless determination to succeed, no matter who he steps on to achieve his goals.

But at the forefront of his actions lies the need for praise, and what better way to stroke his out-of-control ego than to seduce the lonely, bored housewives of upper-crust society and occasionally their willing daughters, or sons, amongst others.

Not averse to broadening his horizons, Roman plays the field while refusing to use gender as a barrier to halt winning the ultimate prize; the hedonistic pursuit of pleasure and sensual self-indulgence.

But with that craving for more, and his wilful refusal to look past his own desires, danger creeps out of the shadows intent on punishing Roman for past mistakes.

Designed to melt your Kindle, this is the combined 'Hot In the City' series by best-selling authors, Zane Michaelson, and Kaylee Rose...enjoy the ride because it's a wild one!

Come closer.

At the sound of her familiar voice, my heart thuds in my chest. She speaks as she always does, with words only I can hear, but as much as I try to convince myself otherwise, I know I'm not imagining it.

She's inside the crumbling shell, just waiting, biding her time. "No!"

Come closer, she repeats.

As desire overrides the urge to run, I realise I want to see her. "Stay away from me."

I mean you no harm, Lucas.

"I don't trust you, Mina."

ACKNOWLEDGMENTS

To my husband, sons, and new daughter-in-law, thank you
for always believing in me.
Life isn't always easy, but we make it work. I will always love
you more.

Gloria Nuckols, thank you for your continued support and
friendship. We may not have a project working right now,
but I'm sure we will put our heads together soon and come
up with something spectacular.

Zane Michaelson, it's hard to believe that it's been four years
since our paths crossed. Thank you for taking a chance on
me then as a blogger and now with our co-writing. I'm
excited to get to work on the surprises we have coming soon.

Michelle Cooper, thank you for keeping me sane and
running Kaylee's Heart and Soul while I focused on writing.
Most of all, thank you for being such a great friend.

Giulia, thank you for your friendship and for teaching me new ways to navigate within the book world.

To my beta readers, all the authors, PA's, readers, and friends who have supported me thank you.

To my editor, Mina, thank you for believing in me and helping to shape this series into something I can be proud of. It was a long, often tear-filled experience, but you didn't give up on me and for that, I will forever be grateful. I couldn't have finished Lance and Kellie's story without your guidance. Thank you for always having my best interest at heart.

THANK YOU
~Kaylee Rose
xoxo

ABOUT THE AUTHOR

Kaylee Rose is a wife, mother, sports fan, and contemporary romance author looking to stretch her creative muscles and explore other genres as well.

Inspired by her husband's career in law enforcement, and her passion for the written word, Kaylee began to pen her novels as an escape from the rigors of everyday life.

Kaylee's series, The Weight of the Badge, was written after attending law enforcement classes with her husband. The seminars focused on the stress a first responder faces daily, how it affects their lives both on and off the job and the continually growing number of law enforcement suicides. With her books and her experience married to a law enforcement officer, Kaylee found herself armed with the perfect platform to use her voice and subtly spread the statistics others may not know. Kaylee Rose is passionate about sharing sexy stories with an important message mixed in.

Kaylee's husband is her biggest supporter, believing in her even when she can not, and writing love stories comes naturally to her after falling in love with him at first sight.

For more information or just to touch base with Kaylee, you will find her at:

Official Website

WWW.AUTHORKAYLEEROSE.COM

RESOURCES FOR OFFICERS

Resources for officers and their family members who may be struggling.

CopLine offers a confidential 24-hour hotline answered by retired law enforcement officers who have gone through a strenuous vetting and training process to become an active listener.
Hotline: 1-800-COPLINE (267-5463)

Safe Call Now is a confidential, comprehensive, 24-hour crisis referral service for all public safety employees, all emergency services personnel, and their family members nationwide.
SAFE CALL NOW: 1-206-459-3020

Under the Shield (855) 889-2348

NATIONAL SUICIDE PREVENTION LIFELINE
1-800-273-TALK (8255)

Made in the USA
Monee, IL
28 June 2022